Alex cast Sarah a
glittering threat of a smile.

"Although I strive hard to pity you for your lack of femininity, your shrewish tongue and your unashamed malice, I do indeed find it a quite extraordinary challenge."

Sarah's loathing for him was magnified into a murderous heat.

"Let us waste no further time. You are telling me that you wish to deprive Nikos of his natural heritage and his father out of spite. I will not allow you to do it. He belongs with my family."

LYNNE GRAHAM was born in Northern Ireland and has been a keen romance reader since her teens. She is very happily married, with an understanding husband, who has learned to cook since she started to write! Her three children, two of whom are adopted, keep her on her toes. She has a very large wolfhound, who knocks over everything with her tail, and an even more adored mongrel, who rules everybody. When time allows, Lynne is a keen gardener and loves experimenting with Italian cookery.

Books by Lynne Graham

HARLEQUIN PRESENTS

LYNNE GRAHAM

GRAHAM

Bond of Hatred

Harlequin Books

TORONTO • NEW YORK • LONDON
AMSTERDAM • PARIS • SYDNEY • HAMBURG
STOCKHOLM • ATHENS • TOKYO • MILAN
MADRID • WARSAW • BUDAPEST • AUCKLAND

ISBN 0-373-11758-2

BOND OF HATRED

First North American Publication 1995.

Copyright © 1995 by Lynne Graham.

CHAPTER ONE

SARAH stood still as a statue at the glass viewing window. Her wide emerald eyes were burning. Every muscle in her body was rigid with tension. Every muscle ached. Only the most fierce self-discipline held back her exhaustion. It had been a long night and a devastating dawn. And every minute, every agonising hour of it was etched into her soul. The nurse wheeled over her nephew's cot and displayed him with a wide smile.

She probably didn't know, Sarah thought numbly. She looked back at the nurse, her fine-boned face ashen and strained, her facial muscles frozen into a mask. The nurse stopped smiling but Sarah didn't notice. Her attention had locked into her nephew. He had a shock of black hair and a pair of furious dark eyes.

There was nothing of Callie in him. He was Mediterranean-dark, his foreign ancestry clearly apparent. He was screaming. He looked so unhappy. She wondered if on some strange wavelength he *knew* that his mother was dead. Dead. She flinched inwardly away from the word and began to walk up the corridor on legs that didn't feel strong enough to support her.

Women didn't die in childbirth these days. Or so she had believed. And Callie hadn't even been a woman in her sister's opinion. At eighteen, Callie had been on the shady boundary line between child and adult. A golden girl with beauty, intelligence and everything to live for... until Damon Terzakis had come into her life and laid it to waste. An immense bitterness gripped Sarah. The emotion was so intense, it literally frightened her.

'Miss Hartwell...'

5

The sound of that voice halted her in her tracks. That dark, accented drawl cut into her like a razor. She shuddered. Slowly she raised her head. He stood several feel away. A male few would overlook. He had to be at least six feet three. His superbly tailored dark grey suit outlined broad, muscular shoulders and long, lean legs. The fabric and the cut alone screamed expense. He had the lethal, inborn grace of a wild animal and the intimidating and instinctive authority of a man born to command.

Sarah stared in disbelief as he extended a lean brown hand. The long fingers, she noticed absently, were beautifully shaped. 'Please permit me to offer my most sincere condolences on your sister's tragic death,' he murmured in a taut undertone.

Sarah took a quick backward step, repulsed by the threat of any form of bodily contact. 'What are *you* doing here?' she demanded shakily.

'You left an urgent message with my secretary,' he reminded her.

'Callie made me phone, but I didn't ask for *you* to come, Mr Terzakis,' Sarah breathed jerkily. 'I asked for your brother.'

'Damon is in Greece.' Alexis Terzakis watched her with impassive eyes as dark as a winter's night. 'I have already informed him of your sister's death. He is most deeply distressed,' he asserted.

A hysterical laugh escaped Sarah. '*Really?*' she gasped incredulously.

'I would like to see my nephew,' Alexis responded, ignoring her response with supreme cool.

'No!' Sarah gritted, her slight body stiffening with a sudden rush of raw aggression that came from fathoms deep down inside her. She hated and detested Alex Terzakis more than any man alive. Her hatred had festered over many months. Now it was like a cancer inside her, eating away until it consumed every other emotion.

'Your right is no greater than mine——'

'*Right*?' Sarah echoed half an octave higher. 'You dare to talk about rights after what you did to Callie? You have no rights over Callie's child, no rights whatsoever! You sicken me!'

'You are distraught,' Alex Terzakis informed her with apparent calm, but she was not fooled. A dark line of blood had risen over his high cheekbones and his mouth had flattened into a pale line.

People did not speak to Alex Terzakis in such a tone. He was fabulously rich and terrifyingly powerful. His minions bowed and scraped. His family walked in awe of him. His word was law. He did not expect opposition. The media had published several bloodcurdling stories about what happened to those foolish enough to challenge Alex Terzakis in business. But Sarah had no fear of him. Sarah would have given twenty years of her life to have the power to *hurt* Alex Terzakis as he had hurt her sister.

'You murdered her . . . you killed her with unkindness. I hope you're satisfied now!' Sarah shot back at him with raw venom.

'Miss Hartwell.' A strong hand caught her wrist as she attempted to walk past him.

'Let go of me, you swine!' Sarah hissed in outrage.

'Were it not for the fact that I am capable of making allowances for your understandable grief, I would demand an apology,' Alex slashed down at her from his imposing height, tiger's eyes raking her enraged face. 'But this is not the place for such a confrontation. Compose yourself before I lose *my* temper!'

Sarah was shivering as though she were caught in a force-ten gale. Outright fury controlled her as he retained that bruising hold on her wrist. She lifted her free hand and hit blindly up at that dark, arrogant face with all her strength. He released her with an incredulous growl, a lean hand flying up to one sculpted cheekbone.

Sarah staggered back. 'Don't ever come near me again!' she slung wildly, dimly shocked by that raw surge of uncharacteristic violence. She could not remember ever striking another human being before. Even as a child she had been a pacifist.

For a split-second, she collided with splintering golden eyes, incandescent with disbelief. And then she tore her gaze from his and forced herself to walk straight-backed down the corridor and out of the hospital.

She was in shock, so deep in shock that she didn't even know where she was going. Callie was dead. She could not yet accept that. Their parents had died in a car crash when Sarah was seventeen. There had been no money. Callie had only been eleven.

'Look after Callie,' her mother had moaned repeatedly in Intensive Care. Mary Hartwell had still been fretting about her youngest child when she'd breathed her last.

Sarah had left school, given up all hope of any further education and concentrated on her sister's needs. She had persuaded her father's cousin Gina to let them live with her. With Gina in the background, the social services had allowed Sarah to keep her sister. Sarah had worked as a waitress. Every day she had come home to cook and clean and tidy up after Gina, who had regarded her as unpaid domestic help and had, in addition, taken almost every penny of her meagre wages.

As soon as she was eighteen, Sarah had found other accommodation. She had done her utmost to give Callie a secure and loving home. She had made her sister her number one priority. And Callie had thrived. A golden girl with the long-legged lithe good looks of a Californian blonde. Smart into the bargain, Sarah observed with helpless pride. It hadn't been easy to keep her lively extrovert sister's mind on the necessity of studying to get on in the world.

But Sarah had managed it. Callie had passed her A levels and gone on to university to study languages. Sarah had been as proud as any mother could have been. She had taken on another job part-time in the evenings so that Callie wouldn't be short of money. Everything had been going so well before Damon Terzakis had entered her sister's life.

'I've met this truly fabulous Greek!' Callie had gushed down the phone. 'He's incredibly handsome and rich and crazy about me...'

'Sounds too good to be true,' Sarah had murmured tautly, disconcerted by Callie's excitement. Callie's boyfriends normally came and went without Callie enthusing about any of them. A beauty from her early teens, Callie had taken young men very much in her stride.

'I'll bring him over to meet you some time soon,' Callie had promised.

But weeks had passed before Sarah had finally met Damon. He had been twenty-five, boyishly good-looking and full of careless charm. His lustrous brown eyes had helplessly followed Callie's every move. He had talked to Sarah as though she were Callie's mother rather than her sister, painstakingly courteous and deferential. By the end of the evening, Sarah had felt like a middle-aged matron of at least fifty.

Damon had gone out of his way to stress that his intentions were serious. Reaching for Callie's hand, he had said, 'I love your sister very much and I want to marry her.'

Behind her polite smile, Sarah had ironically been appalled. She had considered Callie far too young to make such a commitment. She had worried that Callie would abandon her studies outright or, at the very least, allow romance to take over to the detriment of her work. But Sarah had been too sensible to allow her feelings to show. One hint of opposition and Callie was likely to rebel.

Her sister was headstrong and opinionated. Only tact and diplomacy were likely to win Sarah a hearing.

'Of course marriage,' Damon had stated smoothly, 'it would be in the future.'

Sarah had rewarded him with a beaming smile. 'I think that's very sensible,' she had said. 'Both of you have all the time in the world.'

'Don't talk platitudes,' Callie had snapped, withdrawing her hand from Damon's abruptly.

'But we have already discussed this, Callie *mou*,' Damon had protested and, turning his attention back to Sarah, he had added, 'Our love must be seen to have stood the test of time if I am to have any hope of winning my brother's consent to our marriage.'

'Your *brother's* consent?' Sarah had repeated helplessly.

'Greek families function on the basis of a strict hierarchy,' Callie had intervened witheringly. 'At the top of the family pecking order is the dominant male. Damon's father is dead. His brother, Alexis is the big wheel in the Terzakis tribe.'

Faint colour had darkened Damon's good-looking features. He had cast Callie a look of surprisingly strong reproof.

'I don't think you should take cheap shots at Damon's big brother,' Sarah had told her unrepentant sister while she'd prepared supper in their tiny kitchen. 'Or his family. He was offended——'

'Stuff!' Callie had muttered, still angry. 'He's a grown man with a responsible job. But when he talks about Alex he acts like a little boy. He never stops talking about him. Alex this . . . Alex that. You'd think Alex was God in his life.'

'Damon *is* Greek,' Sarah had reminded her gently. 'His culture, his background and his upbringing are bound to differ greatly from yours. If you really love him, Callie . . . all that goes with the territory.'

Sarah surfaced from the past and found herself perched on a bench in the park down the road from the hospital. To think that all those months ago she had actually been *relieved* to hear Damon mentioning the necessity of obtaining his brother's approval before he could marry!

Alarm bells had only really gone off the day she'd caught the name Terzakis on the evening news and glimpsed a forbiddingly handsome male, surrounded by executives and cameras, refusing to comment on his acquisition of some company in New York. She had bought a serious newspaper the next day on the way into work and she had read all about Alexis Terzakis with growing consternation. That evening she had rung Callie and asked her to come home for a night. Callie had come with bad grace, demanding to know what all the fuss was about.

'You said that Damon was running his family's hotel in Oxford,' Sarah had reminded her. 'What you didn't say was that the Terzakis family are billionaires!'

'Alex is the billionaire,' Callie had said drily. 'Damon just gets pocket money.'

'I thought Damon's family were hoteliers——'

Callie had burst out laughing. 'Sarah, you are dumb! Don't you ever read the business columns? Damon's family own a shipping line, an international string of hotels, engineering plants, finance companies...you name it, they own it!'

Sarah had been disturbed. She had genuinely had no idea that her sister's boyfriend was from so wealthy a background. Damon had seemed very unassuming. He had settled that evening into their shabby lounge without a shade of discomfort. She remembered Callie referring to her own job as secretarial and quickly dismissing the subject.

Actually Sarah was a humble filing clerk in a big anonymous office and she had not climbed the ladder any higher because the frequency with which she had held down two jobs had meant that she had no time to spare for evening classes. Sarah had spent countless evenings over the past seven years waitressing or cleaning for extra money to stretch their tight budget.

She had tried not to feel hurt that evening she'd first met Damon when Callie had asked her in advance not to mention those latter sources of income. Callie had been embarrassed by her sister's acceptance of such low-grade employment. And, sadly, Sarah had understood. Callie had always wanted to be *somebody* and that vein of insecurity had been stirred when she'd found herself mixing with students from far more comfortable back-grounds than her own. She hadn't wanted anyone to know that the source of the cheap but fashionable clothes she wore with such panache had been a sister, who regularly cleaned office blocks after closing time.

And now Callie was gone. Sarah raised trembling hands to her face as if she could somehow contain the anguish inside her. She could not imagine life without Callie. Callie with her raw energy, boundless untidiness and quick temper. Callie had been born when Sarah was six. Sarah, a quiet, rather lonely child, had delighted her parents by displaying not the smallest atom of jealousy. She had been enchanted by her baby sister. She had read her stories, picked her up when she fell over, taught her nursery rhymes before she started school and later helped her with her homework. With two parents working full-time, there had been plenty of opportunity for Sarah to fill in the gaps in Callie's days when their mother was too tired or too busy.

'Miss Hartwell.'

Sarah lifted her aching head like a sleepwalker and focused on Alex Terzakis in disbelief. He looked alien against the backdrop of the scruffy park.

'Allow me to offer you a lift home,' he drawled flatly.

Sarah burst out laughing, hysteria clawing like insanity at her cracking composure. Abruptly she covered her working face again, stricken that he of all people should see her in such a state. Dear lord, what did this barbarian want from her now. Couldn't he even leave her to grieve in peace?

Only a couple of hours had passed since she had been bundled unceremoniously from her sister's bedside and the crash team had attempted to get her sister breathing again. It had happened so fast and they had tried so hard. But Callie, once the leading light of her school athletics team, had died of a massive coronary, just days off her nineteenth birthday. Sarah had been shattered but she had been totally devastated by what she'd learnt from the consultant gynaecologist afterwards.

Early in her pregnancy, Callie had been warned that she had a weak heart. Routine testing had revealed what nobody had ever had any cause to suspect. She had been advised to have a termination and she had refused. She had not shared any of that with her sister. Sarah had been surprised by the sheer frequency of Callie's antenatal appointments but she had had no idea that there was anything wrong.

'Callie was one hundred per cent determined to have her baby,' the consultant had told her wryly. 'That was her choice. Possibly she didn't tell you because she was afraid that you might try to change her mind.'

'Miss Hartwell?' Alex Terzakis persisted grimly, impatiently.

Please God, make him leave me alone, she prayed feverishly, curving her arms round her churning stomach and involuntarily rocking back and forth on the edge of the bench.

'I cannot leave you here in this condition,' he continued, his accent growing more pronounced with every unanswered intervention. 'I wish to see you safely to your

home. I also wish to assume responsibility for the funeral arrangements——'

'You bloody savage!' Sarah, who never ever swore,
found the word flying off her tongue. A stricken sense
of horror had attacked her as he'd spoken. 'You wouldn't
let her marry into your family but you can't wait to bury
her!'

'I do not intend to stand here being insulted in a public
place,' he gritted through clenched teeth, and she could
feel the force of his suppressed rage licking out at her
like hungry flames, desperate for fuel to feed on. It was
a curiously satisfying experience, warming her chilled
bones.

'Then you know what to do about it, don't you?'
Sarah collided with blazing golden eyes set between incredibly luxuriant ebony lashes and felt oddly dizzy for
a split-second. She tilted her chin. 'Get lost.'

'If you were not a woman...' he launched at her with
raw, splintering aggression. He was white beneath his
bronzed skin, his classic bone-structure starkly
prominent. He was rigid with fury and frustration.

'You'd be dead,' Sarah murmured shakily. 'If I were
a man, I'd have killed you for what you did to Callie in
your fancy big office five months ago!'

His brilliant gaze had narrowed to piercing pin-points
of light, arrowing over her very small, very slight figure
and the huge green eyes dominating her triangular face.
'On this occasion, I desired only to offer you my assistance at a time of severe trial to us *all*.'

He strode off. Incredibly good carriage, she noted abstractedly, and then it hit her finally. Callie gone...Callie
gone forever. She had not cried a single tear. Her eyes
had burned and scorched but remained dry throughout. And now the tears came in a silent tidal wave,
streaming down her quivering cheeks in agonised relief.
She was so terribly grateful that it hadn't happened in
front of him.

*   *   *

'You'll never guess who just walked in.' Gina nudged Sarah in the ribs seconds after the short funeral service began, her plump over-made-up face suddenly wreathed with rampant curiosity. 'It's *them* ... got to be, hasn't it? Who else could it be?'

'Shush,' Sarah urged, her head downbent as the service opened with a short prayer.

Alex and Damon Terzakis. The combined view of them hit her like a punch in the stomach at the graveside. She went white with outrage, considering their presence a desecration of Callie's memory. How dared they come here and mourn her sister when between them they had made her sister's last months a living hell? How dared they! Damon was studying the ground. He was thinner, older than she remembered, both hands clasped tightly before him.

'Decent of them to come ... the way you feel,' Gina muttered out of the corner of her mouth. She was a large woman in her late forties and an inveterate talker, no matter what the occasion.

People began to leave, shaking her hand. Mostly very young people, Callie's friends from her schooldays. Nobody from the university, but then Callie had abandoned her studies many months previously and broken all contact with the friends she had made there. Without warning, Gina darted from her side and approached the Terzakis males. Infuriated by her defection, Sarah walked on with the minister and parted from him beside Gina's car.

Sickened, she stared at the black limousine with its tinted windows and chauffeur standing by on the other side of the churchyard. She hadn't been able to afford even one funeral car. But then things like that weren't important, she reminded herself painfully, and she had to conserve what little money she had for her nephew.

'I'm going to call him Nikos, after Damon's father,' Callie had announced months ago, after a scan had revealed the sex of her unborn child. She had wanted to know whether she was carrying a boy or a girl and she had been over the moon when she'd learnt that it was a boy.

'Damon won't be able to stay away,' Callie had forecast almost smugly, patting her swollen stomach. 'Not from his son.'

Sarah had been amazed at the strength of her sister's naïve faith in the man who had abandoned her to single parenthood. After all that had happened, she had been unable to comprehend how Callie could still hope, but during her sister's pregnancy she had been reluctant to deprive her of any belief that bolstered her spirits. She had been dreading the aftermath of the birth when poor Callie would have been faced with reality. She would have waited in vain for a proud father to show up. Damon was a wimp, utterly under big brother's thumb, and the threat of disinheritance and exile from his beloved family had completely overpowered his much vaunted great love for Callie!

Gina swam back to her, beaming all over her round face, and unlocked the car.

'Why did you speak to them?' Sarah whispered painfully.

'Because you're being absolutely stupid!' Gina said bluntly. 'If you want to keep that baby, be practical. Bite your lip and let *them* keep you both——'

'I'd sooner be dead!' Sarah exclaimed.

'He's little Nicky's dad, isn't he? Why shouldn't he pay up?' Gina demanded. 'You can bet your bottom dollar that they'll pay a packet to keep all this out of the newspapers.'

'Gina——' Sarah muttered, dismayed but not particularly surprised by the older woman's calculation.

'You've got to be realistic, love,' Gina continued, not unkindly. 'You want little Nicky and I think you're crazy, but then you always were the maternal type, even as a kid. So keep him and raise him and make them pay through the nose for it!'

'I don't want *anything* from them!'

'If you don't take their money, you'll have to live on benefit,' Gina pointed out drily. 'And the social services will pursue Damon.'

'To Greece?' A hysterical laugh was lodged like a sob in Sarah's constricted throat.

'Well, they wouldn't have much trouble tracking him down, would they?'

'I won't take anything from them,' Sarah stated tightly. 'Ever!'

'Callie would have wanted the very best for her son,' the older woman said shortly. 'And I think it's time you faced the fact that Callie knew damned fine what she was doing when she got pregnant.'

'I beg your pardon?' Sarah looked at her father's cousin in shock and reproach.

'It was no accident in my opinion. Callie wasn't that careless. She wanted that boy and when things weren't going as she wanted them to she let herself fall pregnant,' Gina opined wryly. 'Women have been using pregnancy to trap men into marriage for centuries, love. Teenage girls are particularly fond of the method. Unfortunately your sister miscalculated.'

'I disagree.' Sarah had to struggle to hold her voice level and conceal the depth of her anger on her sister's behalf. 'Callie didn't try to *trap* Damon. He had already asked her to marry him, bought her an engagement ring——'

'Talk's cheap, but where was he when the chips were down? Men!' Gina said with rich cynicism. 'He took off for Greece and she never saw him again. He never even answered her letters. Rat! I'd bury the two of them in the back garden with pleasure if it weren't for little Nicky! Mind you, it would be a sinful waste to do away with rat's big brother,' she sighed reflectively. 'Now, he really is gorgeous. Like Apollo the sun god...'

Unused to Gina making mythological references, Sarah stared at the other woman wide-eyed.

Gina flushed slightly as she drew up in front of her small terraced house. 'I went on holiday to Greece once and I saw this statue... Forget it, I'm being silly!'

A neighbour had sat with Nicky while they were attending the funeral. Sarah rushed upstairs to see him. He was fast asleep, snug in his wicker basket. She had brought him home from hospital only yesterday. As she looked down at him, just itching to hold him again, her eyes moistened. In her darkest hours of grief, she had learned to thank God for the gift of Callie's child. She felt needed again and that strengthened her.

Gina was out on the tiny landing. Her plump face was tight. 'If you take that child on, you'll *never* have any life of your own. Didn't you sacrifice enough for Callie?'

'What on earth are you talking about?'

'You're only twenty-four and you've got lonely old maid written all over you!' Gina looked her over in rueful despair, taking in the tightly restrained silver-blonde hair ruthlessly confined in a French pleat, the complete absence of cosmetics, the conservative navy suit that had seen better days and the sensible flat shoes. 'Haven't you ever *wanted* a man in your life?'

Sarah uttered an embarrassed laugh. She hated it when Gina started on about men as if they were the beginning, the middle and the end of a woman's existence. She didn't attract the opposite sex. As a teenager, she had been painfully shy and studious, the class swot. As an adult, she had had neither the time nor the opportunity. Sure there had been men who'd asked her out from time to time at work, and occasionally she had accepted, only to discover that they didn't want her company, they wanted sex. And that was why they had approached her. She was plain and quiet and they had undoubtedly imagined that she would be so grateful for the attention that she would fall into their bed on the first date with the barest minimum of effort.

She made herself recall her painfully humiliating experience with the boy she had had a crush on at sixteen. He had invited her out to a disco one night and she had been electrified with delight...until she'd heard some of her classmates giggling about it in the ladies' cloakroom. He had done it for a bet. Every giggle had been a knife in her heart, every cruel word engraved on her memory for life.

'She looks like an albino.'

'And she's got no boobs at all.'

'You don't need boobs with an IQ like hers.'

'Her IQ didn't warn her that Ashley is setting her up for a bet...She's too busy following him with those big moony eyes of hers...making a real idiot of herself... I wonder how far she'll let him go when he gets her on her own?'

'As if Ashley would *fancy* her! Can you even imagine it?' And everybody had laughed themselves into hysterics at the mere idea.

'Sarah...'

Sarah blinked rapidly and sank back to the present, pale as a ghost. Gina put a hand on her arm and murmured, 'I've asked Alexis and Damon Terzakis back to the house...'

'You've what?'

'Well, somebody had to do it!' Gina muttered. 'You acted as though they weren't there.'

'If you let them in, I walk out,' Sarah swore vehemently.

Slowly Gina shook her head, her troubled gaze clinging dazedly to Sarah's blazing eyes and rigid facial expression. 'Sarah, what's got into you these last months?' she asked in genuine confusion. 'I don't know you like this. It's as if a stranger has taken possession of you——'

Sarah walked on downstairs. 'There's nothing the matter with me, Gina.'

'You used to be the kindest, most gentle girl. A soft touch, I often thought,' the older woman admitted uncomfortably. 'But you've been changing ever since Callie told you she was pregnant. I know how much you loved her. I can understand how you feel——'

'You couldn't,' Sarah cut in, woodenly controlled.

'That boy must want to see little Nicky——'

'If Damon wants to see Nicky, he'll need a court order,' Sarah asserted fiercely. 'I'll fight them every step of the way.'

'But they're coming to the house!'

'Let them. I'll deal with it.'

The bell went one minute later. Gina gave her a pleading glance and then took herself off into the kitchen. Straightening her slight shoulders, Sarah answered the door. Alex Terzakis stood alone on the doorstep. For the first time in her life, Sarah found herself wishing that she were wearing four-inch heels instead of flats. Alex Terzakis towered over her like an apartment block, casting a long, dark shadow.

She took a hasty step back. 'I didn't invite you here. You're not welcome.'

A powerful hand suddenly slammed up against the front door, forcing it out of her loose grasp and flattening it with a crash back against the hall table. The violence of the gesture shook her and instinctively she backed away out of reach. He strode in and closed the door behind him.

'Now we will talk,' he announced, exuding perceptible vibrations of all-male satisfaction.

She had very nearly given him a black eye, she noted with grim amusement, scanning the faint bruise adorning one high cheekbone. Pity she hadn't had sufficient height to do so! Her heart was thudding a frantic drumbeat behind her ribcage. She felt charged with a sensation disturbingly akin to excitement. The tension in the atmosphere was so thick she could taste it.

Since she was not physically capable of ejecting him from the house, she chose to walk into the lounge ahead of him. 'Frankly, Mr. Terzakis, we have nothing to discuss. Where's little rat?'

'Little rat?' He scrutinised her with narrowed eyes.

'Baby brother, the wimp,' Sarah specified with lancing contempt.

'You are the most poisonous woman I have ever met. Would that I had the curbing of that spiteful tongue!' Alex swore in a vicious hiss, one lean hand visibly coiling into a fist.

Sarah laughed for the first time in days, really laughed. Callie had told her a lot about Alexis Terzakis, relaying it in gossip style over the phone in the early days of her romance with Damon. And she was realising that Damon's awed view of his big brother was fatally flawed. Alex was Mr Ice-cool himself in business and in his private life—according to Damon, that was. So why was it that around her he seethed like a volcano ready to erupt?

'*Cristos* . . . On the day of the funeral,' he growled at her from a distance of ten feet. He didn't trust himself any closer. She understood that. 'Have you no decent feelings?'

'About as many as you had when you called my sister a cheap little scrubber to my face five months ago!' Sarah shot back tight-mouthed.

'I did not employ such offensive terminology——'

'You said she was after his money and she slept around . . . Tell me the difference?' Sarah invited with only the slightest tremor in her voice.

'I did not believe she was pregnant,' Alex breathed curtly through perfect white teeth. It was obvious that the admission was wrenched from him.

'I want you to get out,' Sarah told him shakily. 'You have no business in this house.'

He sent her a glittering black glance of startling ferocity and strode over to the window. 'My brother is too ashamed to face you...' he gritted in a driven undertone.

In a weird way, Sarah was beginning to enjoy herself. If the previous admission of faulty judgement had been wrenched from him, the latter had been ripped screaming from Alex Terzakis. Little brother was a wimp. And that offended and humiliated big brother no end! Family honour and all that macho nonsense. Alex was being forced to deal with a woman he despised in a situation in which he had no defence, she registered with increasing confidence. He was here to buy silence.

To buy *her* silence. Maybe he was scared she would talk to the newspapers. He was a very private man, this Greek tycoon with his barbaric arrogance and pride. He detested publicity. And it wasn't a *nice* story, was it? A teenager led up the garden path by a rich, spoilt young playboy and then dumped at spectacular speed once he had had what he had wanted from her. Then that same teenager had been threatened by powerful lawyers, offered hush-money and told to get lost and forget she had ever known anyone with the name of Terzakis!

Sarah's stomach filled with nausea. It was a horrible story but it only became tragedy if you knew that Callie had loved him right to the bitter end. Tears burned her lowered eyelids and she fought them back bitterly.

'If by any means within his power Damon could restore her to life, he would.' She clashed with hard, dark eyes as treacherous as black ice and briefly felt as though she had gone into a skid. The speed with which he had damped down his fury and reasserted rigorous self-discipline sharply disconcerted her. 'But he cannot.

However, he can take charge of his son and give him the life to which he should have been born by right.'

Sarah froze. Her throat closed over. Her long lashes fluttered as she simply stared at Alex Terzakis in disbelief. 'Give h-him the life…?' she stammered in a daze, thrown wildly off balance by the statement. 'What did you say?'

Reading her astonishment, he smiled—he actually smiled. The merest twist of that sensual, perfectly shaped mouth but no less than a smile. 'Naturally, Damon wishes to raise his child in his own home where he belongs.'

CHAPTER TWO

SARAH took several shocked seconds to absorb her incredulity. The Terzakis clan wanted Nicky! They wanted Callie's child! It was a staggering suggestion and she couldn't credit that Alex Terzakis could be serious.

Alex took her silence as encouragement. He studied her as a cat studied a mouse, calculation written all over him. 'Damon adores children. Nikos would be greatly loved.'

'I really...I really don't believe I'm hearing this,' Sarah admitted tremulously. 'You wouldn't let your brother marry her and yet you think he has the right to take her child? He cut her off, ignored her letters, allowed you to humiliate her and let her go through a very difficult pregnancy without any support...and you come here and you tell me that he wants her *baby*?' As she spoke, her shaken voice strengthened with growing anger.

'Whatever you feel for my brother, he *is* the father of your sister's child,' Alex delivered harshly, surprisingly silent and taut in receipt of her condemnation.

'I can't believe that you accept that——'

'Damon inherited a rare blood group from my mother's side of the family. I understand that Nikos also shares that blood group,' he volunteered smoothly, seemingly unaware of the gross offence he was offering by admitting that he had taken up all the evidence available before conceding that Nicky was his brother's child. 'The chances of that occurring by coincidence are several million to one.'

'And you're probably still checking those out!' Sarah slung at him in disgust.

'I am not prepared to be drawn into argument with you, Miss Hartwell.' He angled his gleaming dark head high and surveyed her with innate superiority and un-hidden contempt. 'I am only here for the child's sake as negotiator on my brother's behalf.'

'Negotiator?' Sarah echoed, trying and failing to swallow back her increasing distress.

'Conciliator?' he suggested with black velvet cool. 'The past cannot be changed. We must consider my nephew's future——'

'Nicky's f-future is with me!' Sarah told him, but she was badly shaken by an offer she had never envisaged being made.

'No doubt you think to drive the price up with this pretence of attachment to the child of a father you despise——'

'The price?' she whispered.

'Any price... name it and it is yours,' Alex Terzakis murmured softly, seductively, like a dope dealer dangling death before an addict.

Sarah was so appalled by his estimation of her character that she said nothing.

'You hand over Nikos quietly, discreetly, keep your mouth shut and in return... in return,' he repeated with golden eyes so intent on her that his gaze felt like a physical touch, 'I will give you whatever you want. Think of that. You have had a hard life. What age are you? Thirty, thirty-one?'

Mesmerised, Sarah stared back at him, her trembling hands curving convulsively round a wooden chair-back. Thirty, thirty-one? Dear heaven, did she look that old?

'You could *do* something with yourself,' Alex Terzakis pointed out lazily. 'It's not too late. Money can buy beauty. With concentrated effort and professional advice, you could be quite attractive——'

'You don't say.' Sarah could hardly get out the response. Although she had few illusions about her looks,

any she might have had were being insensitively ripped
to shreds.

'The world could be your oyster. You could travel.
You're a clever woman. You could probably find yourself
a husband.'

Sarah shuddered as she breathed in deep. Desperate
for a man . . . embittered by her lack of one. Clearly that
was how Alex Terzakis saw her. With rigorous determination she suppressed a squirming sense of utter humiliation. He was Greek to the backbone. What Callie
called 'unreconstructed man', what Sarah called a
Neanderthal primitive. He belonged in a cave, not a
civilised society. Or in a museum alongside the dinosaur
display.

Even in the depths of the mortification she was struggling to conceal from him she was conscious of a helpless
current of grotesque fascination. On the surface, he was
so sophisticated . . . but underneath as earthy and as sim-
plistic in his beliefs about the needs of a woman as any
uneducated peasant. He was telling her politely that what
she really needed was a man in her bed . . . Dear lord,
even the dinosaur display would be too advanced for
him! It would never occur to him that celibacy was a
perfectly natural choice for many people.

Then how could it occur to him? Alex Terzakis had
not one but *two* mistresses. One in Athens, one in Paris.
Sarah swallowed back her distaste, repelled by such
rampant and unashamed promiscuity. Evidently his
sexual appetite was voracious and uncontrolled. In today's society, Alex Terzakis was a prehistoric savage,
more to be pitied than anything else, she told herself,
raising her chin. That she should have allowed such a
barbarian to hurt and embarrass her was ridiculous!

'Nicky is not for sale,' Sarah said very drily, but her
cheeks warmed as she dimly questioned her surprisingly
intimate thoughts over the past few minutes.

'I did not suggest that he was but I hardly think that you would wish to tie yourself down with a young and demanding child when you could make a new life for yourself.'

'But I don't want a new life. I am perfectly happy with the one that I have.'

His striking bone-structure tightened, hooded dark eyes resting on her without any perceptible emotion at all. 'Then you force me to be blunt——'

'Oh, I don't think you need forcing,' Sarah opined, sweetly sarcastic as she raked him with unhidden derision. 'I would say that being blunt comes very naturally to you. The challenge would be sensitivity.'

'You are a woman of discernment.' Instead of reacting with the anger she had expected, Alex cast her a glittering threat of a smile. 'Although I strive hard to pity you for your lack of femininity, your shrewish tongue and your unashamed malice, I do indeed find it a quite extraordinary challenge.'

Sarah turned crimson and then white in speedy succession. Her loathing for him was magnified into a murderous heat. Her teeth sank into the soft underside of her lower lip and she tasted the sweet tang of her own blood when what she most wanted was *his*.

'Let us waste no further time. You are telling me that you wish to deprive Nikos of his natural heritage and his father out of spite,' he asserted, icily contemptuous. 'In opposition, what do you offer? A hovel for him to live in! The tag of illegitimacy to carry throughout his life! And the guardianship of a woman who is not of good character. Had you had any decency, you would not have encouraged your teenage sister to continue her relationship with my brother——'

Sarah was trembling with fury. 'What control did you have over your wretched brother?'

'I was not aware of their affair until it was too late. You knew from the beginning,' Alex condemned. 'You played your own part in your sister's premature death——'

'God forgive you!' Sarah was stricken to the heart by the charge.

'And, not content with that tragedy, you now seek to destroy my nephew's future. I will not allow you to do it. He belongs with my family. We can give him everything,' he stressed with harsh emphasis. 'An extended family of supportive relatives, quite apart from a loving mother and father of his own...'

Sarah tensed, her fine brows drawing together.

'The finest schools, a beautiful home, the ability to hold his head high wherever he is and in whatever company. He is a Terzakis.' And to be a Terzakis was evidently the very zenith of anyone's worldly ambition, she translated. She was facing a male fired by a powerful pride in his own blue-blooded, monied heritage. He could probably quote his family tree accurately back at least several generations. Little wonder, she thought, bitterly resentful, that Callie Hartwell, daughter of a factory supervisor and a nurse, had been less than nothing to him. No fancy pedigree there, just good working-class breeding.

Her reflections turned back to something that had puzzled her seconds earlier. She *must* have misheard him. He could not have said 'a loving mother'. He could not have said that.

'Androula would love him as her own. There is neither bitterness nor room for malice in her generous heart. She has had many months to adjust to the knowledge that another woman was carrying her husband's child...'

Sarah was paralysed. Androula...her husband's child? Dear God, Damon had got married to another woman while her poor sister had been pathetically pinning her hopes to an eventual reconciliation! He had actually got married! She was sick to the stomach, barely able to move on a stage to the even more staggering assertion that Callie's no doubt triumphant rival was now most generously prepared to play mother to Damon's illegitimate child...

'Let me g-get this straight.' Sarah formed the plea with an intonation wiped clean of emotion by extreme shock. 'You are asking me to hand over Nicky to Damon and...and this And...'

'Androula,' he filled in obligingly.

'Damon's wife,' she repeated, just to be sure that she could not have misunderstood.

'She is a gentle, loving young woman,' Alex emphasised with unconcealed pride in his freedom to make such a claim.

Not a little scrubber like Callie, Sarah interpreted in a passion of pain. She had not misunderstood. She was so appalled by what he was daring to suggest that only the fiercest discipline kept her nausea under control. That this savage did not even appreciate that he was contravening Sarah's every moral principle underscored how very *sick* the Terzakis clan was in terms of basic decency.

Dear heaven, had Callie lived, would they have approached her to demand her child from her? Would Alex Terzakis have accused Callie of spitefully denying her son the wealth and material advantages which Damon alone could supply? Very probably. This was a male who had treated Callie like dirt from the outset, who had never for a single second even considered the possibility that she might be fit to marry his kid brother...no matter that she was already pregnant with his child. Self-evidently, Alex Terzakis did not even allow for the fact that such a low-class, common person as Sarah Hartwell could even *have* finer feelings!

Callie would have died sooner than hand over her son to Damon's wife. The acrid taste of bile in her dry mouth, Sarah walked over to the phone. 'If you don't get out of this house right now, I intend to call the police,' she told him unsteadily. 'After all, you did force your way in.'

'Is this all you have to say to me?' Alex raked at her incredulously. 'Are you completely without shame? I tell you of Androula's generosity——'

'Generosity—th-that's a good one!' Sarah lifted the receiver, fully prepared to carry out her threat. 'What you have just dared to suggest is so frankly obscene it does not require any further discussion, Mr Terzakis. It is the sickest, most vile proposition I have ever heard.'

'Obscene?' He made it sound like a strange word.

Reluctantly, Sarah forced herself to look at him. Perceptibly she shuddered as she clashed with black ice eyes of enquiry. '*Get out*!' she told him ferociously.

'I have no intention of departing before we reach agreement.' Rock-like resolution emanated from him in teeth-clenchingly arrogant waves.

'If you don't get out,' Sarah swore between clenched teeth, abandoning the phone to employ a far more realistic form of intimidation, 'I'll approach the dirtiest tabloid available and tell *all* . . .'

Absolute outrage paralysed him. Violence shimmered rawly in his brilliant golden stare. 'You would do that to Androula?' he prompted very, very quietly.

A shiver ran down her taut backbone but she stood tall in spite of it. 'I don't give *that*——' she snapped her fingers with a sharp crack '—for your precious, saintly Androula!'

'Were you of my sex, I would break every bone in your vindictive body . . . slowly,' he told her wrathfully.

'You'd get your fingers burnt,' she derided. 'You can't touch me and you know you can't—that's what's making you so angry. If either you or your brother approaches me again, I go to the Press. Damon could have had his child, Mr Terzakis. He had his chance and he blew it. My sister gave her life to bring Nicky into the world.

That's how precious he was to her and that's how precious he is to me!'

'You have no right to keep Nikos!'

'Watch me ... or fight me in court ... where all will be revealed,' she reminded him with satisfaction, now that she had established his Achilles' heel. He was too proud to face the washing of the Terzakis dirty linen in public. 'Damon and his wife will never ever take possession of Callie's child. Accept that and stay out of our lives.'

He was white beneath his sun-bronzed skin, white with savage anger that he was visibly fighting to rein back. '*This*, then, is your revenge——'

'It is not one atom of what I would like to do to you and your family,' Sarah admitted, powered by a surge of helpless aggression. 'Damon was a wimp but *you* are the one who destroyed my sister's life. Why? Because she wasn't good enough...she didn't meet your snobbish standards and she was poor——'

'I am innocent of such prejudice!' he slashed back at her. 'And to use an infant as a weapon of revenge is the true obscenity!'

'Do you know what real revenge would be?' Harshly she laughed, acknowledging that he was unhappily out of her reach. 'It would be making *you* suffer for what you did to Callie. It's your fault that Nicky is illegitimate, nobody else's,' she spelt out. 'Your filthy family pride came before honour and decency. When you said I was not of good character, I should have laughed in your face!'

'*Cristos* ...' With the charged and splintering aura of a wild animal at bay, Alex Terzakis shot a guttural stream of Greek at her, spreading both hands wide in a raking arc of dark, smouldering rage.

'*You* daring to say that to *me*,' Sarah continued, pressing on with the fearlessness of outrage. 'You with your women you have to *pay* to have sex with you! You with your ignorant, chauvinist double standards and sickening hypocrisy! Lay one finger on me, Mr Terzakis, and I will see you in prison with pleasure!'

'Some day... some incredibly lucky man will beat you stupid and teach you respect!' Alex Terzakis swore with two clenched fists.

Sarah was on a high of quite extraordinary energy. The sight of him standing there, seethingly frustrated by a desire to kill her just to shut her up, boosted her adrenalin with amazing efficiency. 'Do you want to know what you really deserve?' she asked with saccharine sweetness, venom dripping from every syllable. 'A wife who would make your life a living hell—a real bitch!'

'Like you?' He vented a cruelly amused laugh, raking her with merciless derision.

'I wouldn't touch you with a barge-pole!' Sarah's face was hectically flushed. 'You are the most utterly repellent man I have ever met,' she said with impressive conviction. 'I may not rejoice in much in the way of physical beauty——' she flung her head high as she made the admission in a small, tight voice '—but my standards are very high, unlike yours.'

He couldn't take his eyes off her. Still as the Greek statue Gina had fancifully compared him to, Alex Terzakis was studying her with almost compulsive intensity. 'No woman has ever found me... repellent.' He could hardly get the word past his compressed lips, he was so outraged by the label.

'Money obviously talks.' Sarah cast wide the lounge door in an open invitation for his departure. For a split-second, she really thought he was going to take a fighting chance at landing himself in a prison cell. He was possessed by the force of his own fury. He smouldered, he vibrated, he emanated violent rage into an atmosphere that positively sizzled, ready to burst into open flames. And all in silence. She discovered that she couldn't take her eyes off him either. Involuntarily she was mesmerised by the sheer passion of so volatile a temperament.

Unexpectedly, he strode past her. And then she realised why. Gina was sitting on the bottom step of the stairs, eyes out on stalks, too shaken by what she had heard even to pretend not to have been eavesdropping.

'You will hear from our lawyers.' The announcement was hissed over one broad, set shoulder halfway out of the front door.

'One visit, one attempt at intimidation, one even mildly threatening letter and I'll sing like a canary for the Press,' Sarah slung before she slammed the door in his wake.

Gina was gaping at her with a dropped jaw. The silence seemed to go on forever.

'I doubt if he will bother us again,' Sarah finally muttered stiffly, wondering just how much the older woman had contrived to overhear.

Slowly Gina shook her head, still staring. 'I just can't believe what I've been listening to... that that was *you* baiting him, taunting him...'

'I handed him a few home truths. That's all. And Mr Ice-cool he's not,' Sarah could not resist savouring. 'I bet every woman he meets fawns on him, feeds his ego...'

'Is that why you felt you had to tell him that he was repellent,' Gina enquired not quite steadily, 'and that he had to pay for sex?'

'I wanted to hit him where it hurt.' But Sarah couldn't meet Gina's gaze. In retrospect, she was ashamed that she had revealed her knowledge of his sex-life but she was not remotely ashamed that she had accidentally stumbled on the brand of attack he found hardest to tolerate.

'I don't believe he has to pay for sex... he's breathtakingly handsome... and you're saying that he consorts with hookers?' Gina probed with rampant curiosity.

'He keeps two mistresses. If he keeps them, he's paying for his pleasure——'

'That's not the same thing at all!'

'Why are you defending him?'

Gina groaned. 'Sarah, he is not responsible for Callie's death. Nobody is responsible for that. You're becoming obsessed. You're hurting, yes,' she conceded, 'but you are taking this all too personally——'

'Losing Callie w-was very personal.' A shuddering sob suddenly trembled through Sarah's slight frame.

Gina put her arms round her in an awkward hug. 'But you have to think of Nicky, love...'

'Are you telling me that you think I *should* hand him over to Damon and his wife?' Sarah asked sickly.

'If his wife is willing and it's not just a front to keep Damon sweet...but then, how could you ever know whether it is or not? Don't look so betrayed,' Gina pleaded, her round face uncertain and engraved with lines of strain. 'I'm all mixed up too. I really don't know what to think any more. But the one thing I *do* feel is that Nicky's welfare ought to come first, and with the best will in the world...how can you match a tenth of what they can give him?'

'Money's not everything,' Sarah protested, distressed by Gina's candour and pierced on her weakest flank by the grudging acknowledgement that Nicky did have the right to a share of the Terzakis wealth...but surely not at the expense of grossly offending against Callie's memory? However, Gina was right... Ultimately, Nicky's needs and future happiness had to be considered first and her own bitter feelings, painful as they were, must not be allowed to colour her response to an offer of a loving, caring home from the other side of Nicky's family.

But, dear lord, Alex Terzakis had accused her of using Nicky as a weapon of revenge when nothing could be further from the truth! If Damon and his wife genuinely wished to bring Nicky up as their child, let *them* come and make that offer personally, let them demonstrate their sincerity and their whole-hearted desire to take him into their family... It was not Alex's job to do their talking for them! And then Sarah might well be forced to think again of what was best for Nicky. In the meantime, Nicky was not some kind of parcel to be posted off into the unknown. Dear God, she *loved* him!

'He's a tiny little baby and I reckon you're going to find him a far heavier burden than you ever found Callie,' Gina sighed. 'You'll have to live here with me. There is no other way.'

The following week was a period of turmoil for Sarah. Nicky was adorable but he didn't sleep very much. He didn't want to eat every four hours either; he wanted to eat constantly. Gina had never had anything to do with babies. She tried to help, but Sarah relied heavily and slavishly on every word of advice advanced by the health visitor. At the same time, she was still struggling to adjust to the reality that Callie really was gone.

The phone rang and she expected it to be Callie. She saw someone with long blonde hair in the street and was jolted. She visited her sister's grave three times in an anguished attempt to teach herself acceptance, but what made her alternately sob and rage most was the anger. And the anger was what she was least equipped to deal with.

Only with Alex Terzakis had she been able to let the anger out. She found that she couldn't open up with Gina. Presumably her hatred for Damon's brother allowed her to vent her true emotions freely, and that was good, not peculiar, *good*, she told herself repeatedly. And he had been a most satisfying target.

One week later to the day, Alex turned up again without warning. Gina was out. It was about eight in the evening. Sarah had just got out of her bath and she was on the way to bed, having decided that the only sensible way to manage was to sleep when Nicky condescended to sleep. When the bell went, she groaned, reckoning it was yet another of Gina's friends, who frequently came round to gossip at night over a long gin and tonic.

But it was Alex Terzakis. Sarah was appalled. One slim hand grabbed at the loose neckline of her faded floral robe, the other frantically attempting to tighten the sash. She was immediately conscious that she was naked beneath the thin fabric, and that both embarrassed and infuriated her. 'What do you want now?' she muttered shakily.

He stepped gracefully past her. 'Five minutes of your time.'

'If you'll excuse me, I'll get dressed,' she enunciated frigidly.

Coming through the door, he hadn't even looked at her. Now he did. Golden eyes wandered a most unwelcome path over her in the dim hall light. 'Why bother?' he drawled flatly. 'It wouldn't bother me if you were stark naked.'

Crimson ran up in a river of colour to her hairline. Her mouth closed tightly. She stalked past him and settled herself down on the sofa without any ceremony. The towel wrapped turban-style round her small head began to fall and with a jerky hand she trailed it off and threw it aside.

A cascade of silver-blonde hair fell in a silky tangle of disarray almost to her waist. He stopped dead in his tracks and dealt her an arrested glance. Sarah searched his suddenly narrowed golden gaze blankly and then looked over her shoulder to see what had attracted his attention. Gina's floral wallpaper covered by blooms the size of dinner-plates? The cuckoo clock?

She turned back to him irritably. For some reason, he still looked riveted and he very narrowly missed tripping over one of the tiny wine-tables which cluttered the room. He snaked out a speedy hand and restored the rocking article, his perfectly shaped mouth twisting with annoyance.

'May I sit down?' He surveyed her expectantly.

'Suit yourself.'

'You could offer me a drink,' he suggested drily.

'You are not a welcome guest, Mr Terzakis.'

Under her stunned scrutiny, he strolled over to the tray of alcoholic beverages on the sideboard, located the whisky, selected a glass and helped himself. 'I should warn you that I find it impossible to be even slightly courteous in your vicinity.'

Sarah took refuge in silence but her nerves were singing like a soldier's on the brink of a battlefield.

He sank down with indolent grace into an armchair opposite and regarded her with utterly unreadable black ice eyes fringed by ridiculously long, luxuriant lashes. 'Last week, I made several miscalculations,' he murmured smoothly. 'It is obvious that you have no intention of giving up Nikos——'

'Nicky,' Sarah slotted in shortly.

'Nicky—how cute.'

But he was saying it, she noted with rich satisfaction.

'No intention of giving him up...am I correct?'

'Very rarely, but on this occasion, yes.' But was that quite true? Sarah had tossed in her bed over several nights, questioning whether she was doing the right thing in utterly rejecting the proposal he had made for Nicky's future. In material terms certainly the Terzakis family had a great deal to offer Nicky, and the further suggestion of *two* parents... But then, it was the potential parents that worried Sarah the most.

'It was perhaps...tactless,' he selected softly, 'of me to suggest that my brother and his wife assume responsibility for him.'

Sarah was not acquainted with him in this mood. She frowned. He was purring like a sensuous cat and toeing the line, a line she had frankly not expected him to abandon so easily. 'Not tactless,' she said. 'Brutally insensitive.'

'The child's future could be secured in another way,' Alex proffered. 'I could adopt him and bring him up as *my* son.'

Sarah was thrown by the proposal, tossed casually at her without the smallest of preliminaries. The tip of her tongue snaked out to moisten her dry lips. His darkened eyes suddenly flamed into gold, his attention dropping to the surprisingly voluptuous curve of her lower lip and lingering. Faint colour threw his hard cheekbones into prominence. He tautened, shifting slightly in the chair, a tiny muscle pulling tight at the corner of his unsmiling mouth.

There was a thrumming tension in the air. She didn't know where it had come from but it unsettled her, brought her skin out in goose-flesh. She stiffened, and watched that so expressive mouth of his suddenly slide into the faintest of smiles. It was there and then it was gone as though she had imagined it, leaving her scrutinising him with uneasy suspicion of she knew not what.

What was the matter with him? Had he been drinking? Perhaps that was why he had to help himself to whisky—dire need rather than simple ignorant bad manners. He *had* nearly fallen, she reminded herself. In addition, he couldn't seem to hold his concentration.

And he wasn't the only one, she registered, although she could scarcely be blamed for losing focus on the conversation when he was behaving so oddly. As for his proposal that *he* adopt Nicky! Barely worth the breath required to answer. No...no...no.

'You would hand Nicky over to your brother. That's what you would do.' She spoke her thoughts out loud.

'I am a man of my word, a man of honour.' Night-dark eyes rested on her again. 'But then I doubt that you believe that. Yet it is imperative that—er—Nicky should be accepted as a Terzakis.'

'Imperative to whom?' Sarah demanded.

'Do you really think that one day that child will be grateful to you for denying him his rightful place in society?'

Sarah paled, bent her head, assailed all over again by doubt and uncertainty which she was determined not to show him.

'Your determination to deny my nephew what my family could give him is wholly selfish,' he derided harshly.

Taut and strained, Sarah studied the carpet at her feet. Was it selfish? She was greatly disturbed by the accusation. Didn't he see that from her side of the fence the Terzakis men were a particularly abhorrent yardstick by which to measure the rest of his family? Damon: weak, cruel and uncaring, as revealed by his treatment of her sister. Alex: ruthless, arrogant and equally cruel and un-caring of those less fortunately placed in the world. She did not seek to retain custody of her nephew out of re-venge and respect for Callie's memory alone. No, indeed ...

A child needed more than wealth and status to thrive. A child needed time, understanding and love to grow into a responsible adult. Was it even reasonably possible that Nicky would find those needs fully met by the Terzakis family? Sarah thought not, but she desper-ately wished she had a crystal ball to see into the future because she was frightened by the fear that she could be making the wrong decision on Nicky's behalf. And if that was true, she would never forgive herself ... and Nicky might never forgive her either, she reflected painfully.

She cleared her throat and lifted her head, sure on one point. 'I wouldn't trust you with Nicky. He's a helpless little baby and you're a self-centred workaholic shark who would probably dump him in the full-time care of a nanny——'

The long fingers of one lean brown hand flexed. 'Your insolence astounds me,' he admitted in a roughened undertone.

Ironically, Sarah had merely been honest. For once she had not sought to offend deliberately. She had simply been truthful. 'And what would happen when you married?' she continued doggedly. 'Nicky would get a stepmother who would very probably resent him and favour her own children over him.'

'By what right do you dare to pass an opinion on my character?' he demanded, springing upright with the restive energy of a prowling tiger.

Sarah tensed. One word of criticism and he was on the brink of explosion. 'And then,' she added helplessly, 'there's your temper——'

'My *temper*?' he repeated with a stark flash of grinding white teeth.

'You appear to have little control over it,' she murmured. 'Children can be very trying. They can test your patience to the utmost.'

'You know nothing of my temper!' he intoned, incensed. 'I am a very disciplined man.'

Sarah elevated a brow. 'Oh, I expect you're an absolute pussycat as long as everybody around you is bowing and scraping and you're getting your own way.' She rose to her feet, hoping he was on his way out. 'What you cannot handle is opposition from a mere female...'

A pin-dropping silence stretched. Hooded dark eyes regarded her almost slumbrously. 'I could handle you with one hand tied behind my back... but you wouldn't like my methods.'

For some reason the full onslaught of that disturbingly intent dark stare made her breath catch in her throat. Something deep in the pit of her stomach tightened almost painfully. Her breasts felt curiously heavy. Time seemed to have slowed down. And then he turned his head away, tautening, and strode over to the door.

'Nikos is crying,' he informed her flatly, as though that in itself were an offence.

'Nikos?' Blinking in confusion, Sarah had to dredge herself out of the strange spell she had fallen under for a few dismaying seconds. Involuntarily she shook her head. It was tiredness, stress. Little wonder she was feeling odd.

With a stifled sound of raw impatience at the slowness of her response, Alex strode out of the room and up the stairs, but he hung back for a split-second to breathe in a tone of forbidding censure, 'A baby should never be left to cry.'

CHAPTER THREE

ALEX had already lifted Nicky by the time Sarah reached the bedroom. Her nephew was howling at the top of his lungs, his adorable little face scarlet with misery. Sarah's heart clenched at the mere sight of him. He looked so pathetic.

'Let me take him,' she said, reaching out instinctively for him, eager to proffer all the comfort that any baby could possibly require.

Alex cast her a coldly amused glance. 'I do know what to do with a baby. How often do you leave him to cry?'

Fury coursed through her. 'I never leave him to cry!'

'In my home, he would have instant attention every hour of the day,' he informed her.

Sarah's teeth ground together. 'If you put him down, I'll go and heat his bottle.'

'I will remain here with Nikos until you return.'

That totally *bloody* man! Sarah banged about the kitchen, furious that Alex Terzakis was actually holding Callie's child in his arms! She refused to recognise the bond of blood between them. Neither brother had any right to such an acknowledgment, she told herself.

All of a sudden she was reliving the past again, hugging her bitterness to her like a warm blanket to ward off the freezing chill of Alex's presence in the house.

Seven months ago, Damon had gone over to Greece on business. He had known then that Callie was pregnant, had, according to Callie, been absolutely delighted at the news. Callie had naturally suggested that surely it was time for Damon to introduce her to his brother. With that whopping engagement ring on her

42

finger and Damon's child on the way, hadn't Callie had
every excuse to have expectations of a quick marriage?

Damon had promised to speak to his brother while he
was at home. He had returned, pale and hunted-looking,
shorn of his usual insouciance. Alex was immovable, he
had told Callie. Alex was not even prepared to meet her.
Only then had Callie informed Sarah that she was
pregnant. She had dragged Damon with her to make that
announcement and Sarah had endured an evening of
hideous embarrassment.

No doubt she had been terribly naïve but she had not
realised before that evening that Callie and Damon were
sleeping together. In the same way she had not known
that Callie was actually living with Damon in the
apartment he had taken in Oxford. Callie had concealed
that fact from her, passing off her change of address
and phone number as a move to a cheaper flat with other
girls.

'I am not in a position to marry Callie at this moment
in time,' Damon had informed her stiffly.

'Alex is threatening to cut him off without a penny!
Have you ever heard of such melodrama in this day and
age?' Callie had demanded hotly.

Damon had not been able to meet Sarah's questioning
gaze. Finally, when he could no longer bear the silence,
he had said almost pleadingly, 'I cannot defy my
brother... at least, not at present.'

And Sarah's heart had sunk. It had been an excuse
and not a good enough one in the circumstances. Callie
had become hysterical. Sarah suspected that somehow
her kid sister had expected her to be able to wave a magic
wand and make everything fine again. But the reality
had been that Damon was a grown man. If he did not
have the courage to stand up to his tyrannical brother
and forge his own path in life until such time as his family
came round to accepting his choice of bride, nobody
else could give him that courage.

A week later, Damon had taken off for Greece again with very little warning.

'Did you know that he was going?' Sarah had asked her sister worriedly.

'Don't worry... he'll be back. He really wants this baby,' Callie had asserted doggedly, seemingly unconcerned by the suspicions assailing Sarah.

Sarah had gone over and over Damon's demeanour that evening in her own mind, wondering if it was wickedly cynical of her to suspect that the young Greek was no longer quite so sure of his feelings for her sister. He had not reiterated his once dramatic assurances that he loved Callie. His strain and the alteration in his behaviour had been pronounced. She had not wanted to worry her sister with her fears.

But a fortnight later a suave lawyer had turned up at Damon's Oxford apartment and served Callie with a notice of eviction. Callie had run home to Sarah, outraged by what had happened but convinced that the eviction could not possibly have had anything to do with Damon. It was, she'd insisted, a stupid misunderstanding with the landlord. She had refused to return to university. Sarah had pleaded with her but Callie had refused to listen to her.

In despair, Sarah had decided that perhaps it was her duty to confront Alex Terzakis and attempt to reason with him. Callie had asked her to do it but Sarah hadn't wanted to do it. Only her sister's unblemished faith in Damon had persuaded her. She had been pleasantly surprised when Alex's very correctly spoken secretary had come back to her within the hour with his agreement. He would meet them the next time he was in London.

She remembered that day in his office. It had been unforgettable. Now that day he *had* intimidated her. Right from the first moment she'd laid eyes on him, her stomach had churned. She had gone in good faith to that meeting, angry and defensive on Callie's behalf, but so foolishly certain that when he met Callie he would realise that his prejudice against her was unreasonable.

But Alex Terzakis had never actually *met* Callie. He had let the two of them enter his palatial office and had then fixed his attention solely on Sarah. 'I think that you and I should talk alone, Miss Hartwell.'

A chill ran over her flesh, remembering that instant. He had been so very clever about it. She had not realised that the room he smoothly showed Callie into was about to be invaded by two nasty lawyers, set on frightening her sister to death. Divide and conquer. He had deliberately separated her from Callie.

And Sarah had been so stupid; she had been relieved by Callie's removal from the proceedings, believing that she would be able to talk more freely without her sister's presence and assuming that Callie would be invited back in once the trickiest part of the confrontation was over.

Alex had lounged back in his imposing chair behind his equally imposing desk and murmured silkily, 'You have my full attention, Miss Hartwell.'

'I'm here to ask what you find so objectionable about my sister,' Sarah had framed tightly. 'And why you refused even to consider meeting her.'

An ebony brow had elevated, a sardonic smile that was incredibly chilling curving his mouth. 'That you should even ask that question tells me much. I have no desire to meet your sister. I merely want her out of Damon's life.'

'You haven't answered my question,' Sarah had persisted.

'Why should I?' he had countered with unvarnished insolence. 'Your sister shared a bed with my brother... that is all.'

'He asked her to marry him...'

He had shot her a blatant look of ridicule, backed by cold aggression. 'Pillow-talk... what else? This is not the nineteenth century, Miss Hartwell. Damon is Greek and his blood runs hot. He is also very young——'

'So is Callie!' Sarah had gasped in outrage. 'And she is also pregnant.'

'I don't believe that. I don't think either of you is *that* stupid,' he had dismissed without hesitation.

'Callie is expecting your brother's child——'

'I cannot see where you imagine this claim could possibly lead,' he had interrupted very drily. 'And I had hoped that you would have the intelligence to know when you are beaten. The bird that lays the golden eggs has flown, Miss Hartwell. He's back in Greece and he's staying there. His affair with your sister is finished.'

'Because you threatened him!'

'I have never threatened my brother in his life. Damon knows what is expected of him,' he had asserted grimly, subjecting her to a contemptuous appraisal. 'And a calculating little bimbo with her eye firmly fixed to his wallet never had any hope of turning Damon from what he knows to be his duty.'

Shocked by his insults, Sarah had burst into speech in defence of her sister's character and reputation. And Alex Terzakis had thrown back his dark head and laughed scornfully.

'Your sister, young though she may be, was no virgin. Indeed I understand that she was rather free with her favours long before Damon met her, and not noticeably faithful while he was with her either.'

'How... dare... you?' Sarah had leapt to her feet, affronted beyond belief by his attack on Callie's morals.

'I'm calling your bluff, Miss Hartwell. If we are to talk of daring, I marvel that you had the impertinence to come here. A word of advice,' he had purred silkily, indolently amused by her distress. 'The next time you help your sister to get her claws into a rich Greek, tell her to keep her mouth shut about her previous lovers. Greek men are notoriously backward when it comes to female liberation. They always like to be the first with a woman, or at least to be allowed to pretend they are.'

Dumbstruck by his insolence, she had simply stood there until she'd finally unpeeled her tongue from the roof of her mouth. 'You foul-mouthed——'

'And if she wants that wedding-ring, tell her to keep her legs firmly locked together until she gets to the church. Moving in with Damon was her second mistake.' Glittering golden eyes had dwelt on her shattered face with cruel satisfaction. 'You can get out now. I've said all I want to say.'

Callie had been sitting in tears in the reception area, trembling and equally shaken, clutching a cheque for an enormous sum of money. Sarah had torn it up and thrown it in the bin and it had been hours before she was able to get the full story out of Callie. But one thing Callie had said was, 'They made me feel dirty, Sarah...they made me feel like a blackmailer!'

That tremulous confession was engraved on Sarah's soul like an acid burn. Her sister had been faced with two lawyers, who had proceeded to threaten her with nebulous but, to a teenager, terrifying repercussions should she ever feel tempted to talk about Damon to the Press.

Callie might have bounced back relatively fast from that day. Sarah hadn't. Callie had continued to write to Damon, angry when she got no replies but amazingly not losing hope. 'I bet my letters are being stopped before he gets them,' she had decided. 'I wouldn't put anything past Alex Terzakis. Just wait until my son is born. It'll be a different story then. Nothing will keep Damon away from me.'

The loathsome memory of that day lived for Sarah again now. The hatred came back, borne on a seething tidal wave of bitterness. She paused on the threshold of Nicky's bedroom.

An unexpected scene met her eyes. Alex was reclining on her single bed with her nephew closely cradled against him. He was talking to him in Greek and Nicky was no longer crying. In fact he was making those endearing little snuffling sounds that signified that his attention was being fully engaged. Sarah's stomach heaved at the deceptive imagery.

Alex looked so *human*. But his treatment of Callie had been inhuman. And now he wanted her child, simply expected him to be handed over like a parcel. Why? Nicky was also Nikos, with all that that implied. He was a Terzakis. Incredibly, Callie had correctly estimated the worth of her unborn child to the Terzakis family.

But Sarah was still astonished by the strength of their interest in Nicky. Or should she instead be astonished by the strength of *Alex's* interest? For it seemed to Sarah that Damon's professed desire to bring up his own child had been incredibly short-lived and very easily silenced. So how sincere could the offer have been in the first place? Sarah was chilled by the suspicion that Damon might have been bullied into making that offer more to impress his big brother than out of any real wish to take possession of his son.

Was it fear of public exposure at some future date which made Alex demand custody of her nephew? Some sort of paranoid possessiveness? It was certainly not a question of honour or conscience. Callie's experiences made that clear. Sarah stared at the man and the child, one whom she loved and one whom she hated, and she trembled with the force of her own frustration.

Yes, she did want revenge. An eye for an eye, a tooth for a tooth and all that. She wanted, she *needed* to hurt Alex Terzakis but she could not. It was not within her power. But never at any stage had she not considered Nicky's welfare as being of paramount importance. In scorching silence she removed the baby from Alex's hold, careful not to touch any part of him. She sat down on the chair and began to feed her nephew.

Alex sprang off the bed. 'You must accept that Nikos does not belong here.'

Her teeth gritted. Act two, scene five. He was remorseless and so far he had yet to convince her that anyone in the Terzakis family genuinely wanted Nicky, and surely not all the money in the world would make up for the absence of love? It wouldn't, would it? she asked herself anxiously, torn in conflicting directions by her desperate desire to keep the baby that she had already learned to love and the worrying fear that her own feelings might be too deeply involved to allow her to make a fair, clear-headed decision about what was best for the tiny child in her arms.

'It would be less disturbing for you both if you gave him up now.'

What was he going to offer her now? He had tried money. He had tried intimidation. He had tried very briefly to portray Damon and Androula as perfect parents. And he had finally offered himself. But if Nicky went to Greece, Sarah would have no further say over what happened to him, and how far could she trust any Terzakis male?

'I am not a patient man,' he breathed harshly.

'Tell me something I don't know.'

Fierce dark eyes stabbed into her. The silence stretched and simmered for long minutes.

'I am a dangerous enemy,' Alex finally assured her icily. 'No matter what the cost, I will take that child from you.'

She had finished feeding Nicky. She settled him back down into his cot, desperately striving to conceal the unsteadiness of her hands. How dared he come to her home and threaten her? Hadn't he and his brother between them already done enough damage? The Terzakis men had *killed* her sister.

Damon should have told Callie that he no longer loved her. Instead he had run away, leaving her poor sister to hope in limbo. What had those months of stress done to her weak heart? And what might have been the result had Damon kept his promises and married her? Callie might well have lived.

'Listen to me...' Alex demanded abruptly, closing a strong hand on her arm.

Sarah jerked away violently and started down the stairs. 'Keep your filthy hands to yourself! I can't bear you to touch me,' she hissed.

'Liar.'

She spun round in the hall in a furious turmoil of emotion. Alex Terzakis lounged back against the wall, exuding a blaze of devastating sexual awareness. She had never seen that in a man before. She saw it now, recognised it on some atavistic level not previously explored inside herself. Raw sexuality sizzled from him, in the tautened poise of his lean, hard body, in the smouldering depths of the golden eyes sliding over her and the audible fracture in his breathing pattern.

'I think you would like me to touch you,' he positively purred.

In complete confusion, Sarah backed away from the heat and the suffocating tension that had entered the atmosphere. Her skin felt hot and stretched over her bones. Her body felt strangely weighted and unfamiliar. She translated the sensations as fear. He scared her.

'You're an animal,' she whispered with a shudder.

He dealt her a slashing smile full of all-male triumph as he absorbed her retreat, and she wanted to knock his teeth down his arrogant throat. Calling him an animal was an insult to animals. But he did belong in a cage. Clearly he thought he was irresistible. But what enraged her most was that he was baiting her on a level she could not match.

'Unfortunately when I told you that I would give you whatever you want,' he drawled in a dark, deep voice with an unbelievably insolent smile, 'I wasn't including myself in the offer... When I go to bed with a woman, I have to like her. That is the barest minimum requirement.'

If Sarah had had a knife in her hand, he would have been bleeding to death at her feet. In fact she marvelled that he had managed to reach thirty-three unscathed by vengeful female hands. That he could have the brazen effrontery to insinuate that she found *him* attractive! That he could then go on to suggest that, had he been willing, she would have dropped gratefully into his arms... Frankly, the power to vocalise simply failed her.

He uncoiled himself fluidly from the wall. She shivered. Her hands itched. He made her feel...he made her feel so *violent*. He incited her to violence...his every move, his every word, his every smile. He was a walking incitement to a crime of passion. And yes, he had told her to name her price for Nicky and it would be hers. However, he wasn't likely to walk voluntarily over the edge of a cliff.

But she knew suddenly with crystal-clarity and embittered frustration what the best punishment of all would have been...what would really hurt Alex Terzakis the most. To be forced to marry *her* to gain access to Nicky. A choky little laugh escaped her. Not that he would have agreed, of course, but how perfect a revenge that would have been. An insane idea, but oh, what a beautiful fantasy! Though why should it be a fantasy? a little voice asked. She should make that demand. It would at the very least get rid of him.

Questioning dark eyes, cool as a winter wind, rested on her. 'I am glad that you find something amusing in this situation. I confess that I do not.'

Sarah sent him a veiled glance of pure poison. 'You did ask me to name my price for Nicky... didn't you?'

'I wondered how long it would take for you to abandon the loving aunt act,' Alex admitted, sending her a shimmering look of distaste. 'Why did you waste my time with such a pretence?'

She had never come across anyone whose reactions were more impossible to predict. He talked as though he would give anything, do anything to get Nicky. But when success appeared to beckon he froze and surveyed her with judgemental revulsion. And he hadn't even touched the tip of the iceberg yet, she reflected with bitter amusement.

She took a deep breath. 'You're not going to like my price,' she sighed, strolling into the lounge, wanting to give him a little more space before he lost his temper and exploded. She just *loved* watching him fight for self-restraint.

'I do not care what it costs to remove you from that child's life forever,' he asserted icily.

'But, you see, it wouldn't do that.' Sarah turned back to face him, emerald eyes gleaming with provocation and unconcealed challenge. 'Just how much do you want Nicky, Mr Terzakis? You see, the only thing I want is what you wouldn't let my sister have...'

His gaze had narrowed but it was obvious that he hadn't yet caught her drift. 'Get to the point.'

'It's a little...delicate.' Sarah was electrified by the sense of power he had given her.

'You are no shrinking violet,' he gritted with blistering impatience.

'I want you to marry me.' Sarah dropped it like a brick into a bottomless silence. 'I want to be Mrs Alex Terzakis. In name only, of course,' she added, gently ironic. 'Hard as you may find it to believe, I find you highly resistible. The immense sacrifice of lying back and thinking of the greater glory of Greece would not be required from you.'

As she stopped speaking, she could not believe that she had actually said all that to him. But his unnatural stillness, the dark rise of blood accentuating his carved cheekbones and his stunned silence confirmed that she had. He was transfixed to the spot.

'*Cristos* . . . you think that *I* would marry *you*?' he demanded ferociously.

'A fate worse than death, but so sweet a revenge,' Sarah pointed out softly. 'Am I to assume that I am even less acceptable than my poor sister? Well, you did ask me what I wanted——'

'You cannot be serious . . . you are joking!' Alex sent her a black intimidating glower of expectancy. 'You could not ask such a thing of me and be serious——'

'I could,' she confirmed, revelling in his unwillingness to believe. Alex Terzakis in shock—what a glorious vision.

'What kind of a woman are you that you can ask this of me?'

'So, you are *not* a man of your word.' Sarah savoured the condemnation, her jewel-like eyes shimmering over the sudden perceptible clenching of his golden features with helpless satisfaction. No, he didn't like that—tough.

Alex Terzakis asked for everything he got. This past fortnight had been a nightmare for Sarah, a long, dark tunnel she'd had to force herself to keep on walking through. From the very hour of Callie's death, this arrogant Greek had tormented her and intruded on her grief. Her sister's death had meant nothing to him. Indeed it might well have been a relief. Yet he had dared to appear at Callie's funeral, and on the selfsame day had offered her money in return for her sister's baby. And still he was refusing to leave them alone!

'It is out of the question,' he drawled with unflinching candour. 'But if it is possible I despise you even more for making such a demand.'

Sarah was bitterly amused by his response. Did he really imagine that she gave two hoots what he thought of her? He strode out to the hall, perceptibly eager to be gone.

'Goodbye,' Sarah said drily.

Without warning, he swung back to her, glittering dark eyes shooting over her, the faintest crease drawing his ebony brows together. 'Did you demand marriage for the child's sake?' he prompted tautly, abruptly.

She really had shaken him up. Shorn of his usual sardonic aura, he looked forbiddingly serious.

'What do you think?' His question had thrown her, since she had only been playing a game with him by demanding the one thing that he would not give.

'That revenge is a two-edged sword.'

Moments later she watched the limousine drawing away, accompanied by fluttering curtains on the other side of the street. She fell into bed, totally drained by exhaustion. How *could* she have asked him to marry her? To watch him break out in a cold sweat at the prospect of being tied to an unfeminine, malicious shrew? His opinion of her was immaterial, she reminded herself. His shattered reaction to her proposal had really been quite funny. Absently, she wondered why she wasn't laughing ...

The following week, Sarah went back to work to complete the statutory two weeks' notice required if she was to receive a full month's pay. And she couldn't afford to lose that money. Gina's neighbour, a registered childminder currently without any other charges, took over Nicky. Sarah found it an appalling wrench leaving him every morning.

'You can come and work for me at the shop,' Gina announced over breakfast at the end of the first week.

Sarah felt awful. Gina, who owned a florist's shop, was very fussy about employing only trained staff. 'But I know nothing about flowers——'

'You can learn, but you can start by sorting out all the paperwork. Nicky can come with you. You can stick his basket in the back room.'

'I don't know what to say,' Sarah muttered awkwardly. 'I'm very grateful.'

'I gave you no help with Callie,' Gina sighed, 'but I think we should all stick together this time. I kind of like the company round the house and, although things are a bit frantic right now with Nicky being so young, that'll soon settle down. He'll be off to school before we know it.'

'Do you think I'm doing the right thing...keeping him?' Sarah finally had the courage to ask outright. She so badly needed to hear someone telling her that she was.

'I think you're doing what you have to do,' Gina said nebulously. 'Anyway, it's all up to *them* now, isn't it?'

'How?'

'Well, sooner or later Damon is surely going to roll up on the doorstep and if you want my advice you let him see Nicky without any argument. Nicky has a right to know his father.'

Sarah stiffened and then bit her lower lip. Nicky did have a right to know his father, she acknowledged ruefully...but then she was still waiting for Damon to beat a hot, enthusiastic trail to their door, eager to meet his baby son.

'Mind you, I would've thought he would have shown up by now,' Gina remarked, speaking aloud Sarah's own thoughts on the subject.

Late morning, Sarah became aware of the subdued murmur of voices that usually distinguished the office abruptly rising to a much more noisy level and then suddenly falling very, very quiet. She was in the file-room where she spent most of her working day.

Someone cleared his throat. She spun round and was transfixed by the sight of a phalanx of the top-floor executives all standing out in the corridor staring in at her as though she had grown horns. Her dismayed eyes fell on the managing director, Mr Soames.

'Miss Hartwell...?' he began uncertainly, for he didn't know her, had certainly never spoken to her before.

The executives parted like the Red Sea as another figure strolled into view.

'I came to take you out to lunch,' Alex Terzakis drawled.

'It's n-not my lunch-hour.' Scarcely crediting the scene before her, unable even to absorb his announcement, Sarah answered automatically.

Mr Soames paled. 'Nonsense, Miss Hartwell...you're free to go whenever you like. Take the rest of the day off if you want,' he hastened to add with a strained smile.

Sarah focused on Alex. With effortless ease, he dominated, the sole male in the group who didn't look as though he was standing barefoot on a bed of nails. In a navy pinstripe suit of exquisite tailoring, he had a dark exotic splendour that was undeniably riveting. For an instant she collided with night-dark eyes and she couldn't breathe, couldn't move.

'Miss Hartwell no longer works here,' Alex murmured. 'I have other duties for her.'

'A truly excellent employee,' the managing director rushed to assert heartily.

What the heck was going on? Her cheeks crimson, Sarah moved forward, but before she could speak Alex had planted a hand like an iron bar to her rigid spine and pressed her out of the room. 'You have things to collect?'

'Yes, but——'

He turned his dark head. 'Have Miss Hartwell's desk cleared and her possessions conveyed to her home.'

Somebody said, 'Yes sir.'

She was thrust into the lift in a state of furious bewilderment. 'What the heck are you playing at?'

'I just sacked you.' Alex stared down at her, his handsome mouth tightening. 'You have appalling dress-sense——'

'*You* sacked me?'

'I own this company,' he advanced carelessly, frowning again. 'And as for that hairstyle——'

'*You* own this company?'

'I came here merely to take you to lunch. I was intercepted in the foyer. Someone recognised me and total panic reigned because I have never been here before.' His wide mouth twisted and suddenly he pulled her forward and released the clasp imprisoning her hair before she could even guess his intention.

Filled with consternation and confused by everything he had said and done since his descent, Sarah made a pointless grab at the descending tangle of silver-blonde strands. 'Have you gone crazy?' she gasped.

'I refuse to be seen out in public with a woman who resembles a prison wardress.'

'You sexist pig!' Sarah spluttered. 'In one breath you tell me you've sacked me, and in the next you tell me you're taking me to lunch. I wouldn't eat with you if I was starving!'

'Don't tempt me...' he murmured drily.

'And you're wasting your time sacking me. I was leaving anyway and I already have another job——'

'And it is so difficult to think of you saying anything with flowers that anyone in their right mind would want to hear,' he slotted in silkily. He was forging a passage through the foyer, leaving her simply to bob in his wake.

'How did you know I'm going to work for Gina?'

'She told me.'

'When?' A swing door almost hit her in the face as he strode through it. Fuming, Sarah stopped dead centre of the pavement. 'Your manners are atrocious!'

He paused, flashing her a vibrantly amused smile that quite transformed his usually grim features. On the brink of moving on, she stilled and stared, an odd tightening sensation making its presence felt in the pit of her stomach. Her mouth ran dry. For the very first time, it occurred to her that Gina was right. He *was* extravagantly handsome.

'You called me sexist. Only a sexist would open doors for a woman.'

Sarah slid with the stiffness of a clockwork doll into the rear of the opulent limousine. What did he want this time? Maybe he was planning to give her a pair of concrete boots and toss her in the Thames. A very real sense of unease assailed her. Alex Terzakis kept on overturning her every expectation. He was totally unpredictable. Although she prided herself on being a reasonable judge of character, she had to admit that she had not a clue what went on inside his head but she suspected that a lot of it would be complex, cunning and free of all conscience.

'Would you like a drink?'

Hastily she shook her head.

'Not even to celebrate your triumph?' he drawled, his accent thickening noticeably over the syllables of that final word, his strong dark face clenching.

She studied him suspiciously. 'What triumph?'

'I will pay the price,' he delivered harshly, scanning her with flat dark eyes.

'W-what price?' she began and then fell silent, her throat closing over as she stared at him wide-eyed and stunned.

'I will marry you.'

CHAPTER FOUR

WHATEVER Sarah might have expected it had not been *that*. Not in her wildest dreams had she imagined that Alex Terzakis might accept her provocative and facetious demand and actually agree to marry her. Astounded by his capitulation and conscious of his hard scrutiny, she concentrated fiercely on keeping her face bland and uninformative. But her heart was pounding crazily in her eardrums and shock was reverberating through her in waves. She had demanded the most outrageous price she could think of... and he was prepared to give it to her. Why? Why? she wanted to know. Why was Nicky so important to the Terzakis family? Presumably he had to be the first grandchild and he was male, but surely Damon and his precious wife would quickly produce children of their own? Why would Alex agree to a forced marriage with a woman he despised when the most that sacrifice could gain would be *his* adoption of Nicky?

She chose her words carefully, determined to reveal nothing of her thoughts. 'It would appear that Nicky is worth his weight in gold.'

'*Dios* ...' Alex ground out and her head spun back to him.

She clashed with black ice eyes and a chilly hand closed over her heart, sudden fear clenching her muscles. It was instinctive but she was powerless to translate the sensation into any form of suspicion. Her own fear was simply there, thickening the atmosphere.

'To you, I meant,' she extended tightly. 'You can hardly blame me for expressing my surprise. Callie was four months pregnant when she was evicted from your brother's apartment in Oxford——'

'*Cristos*... do you think I would have made that instruction had I believed your claim that she was pregnant?' With one lean hand, he made a slashing movement of frustration. His dark features were pale and set.

So the eviction *had* been his idea and not Damon's. Once more, Callie had been proved correct in her assumptions. Sarah stared at Alex Terzakis with unashamed loathing.

'What sort of a man do you think I am?' he demanded savagely.

'A complete bastard,' Sarah murmured helplessly from between compressed lips.

'Had I believed that she was carrying my brother's child, I would have behaved very differently,' he emphasised from between gritted even white teeth.

'Oh, I don't think so. The cheque would have covered the cost of an abortion... I don't think you were too concerned either way——'

'How dare you?' The atmosphere burst into flame with the sheer force of his fury. 'There was no such thought in my mind. I would have played no hand in murdering my brother's child!'

Surprisingly she found that she believed him. Surely he could not manufacture such outraged disbelief to order? She bowed her head. 'I gather Damon didn't tell you that she was pregnant.'

'He did not.' The confirmation was stark, dredged from him.

So there had been lies, Sarah registered in disgust. She wondered how many other lies Damon Terzakis had told to save face with his brother. No doubt Damon had also been responsible for Alex's belief that Callie was promiscuous and greedy for money.

'We'll have lunch at my town house.'

Was she so awful-looking that he couldn't bear to be seen in public with her? That was her first thought and swiftly she stamped on it, reminding herself that, unlike him, she was not hung up on physical appearance. In any case there were far more important things to dwell on. He was prepared to marry her...was she prepared to marry *him*?

The town house was part of an imposing Georgian terrace which overlooked a quiet square. Lunch was swiftly served in a lofty-ceilinged dining-room by a uniformed Greek maid. Alex's silence was starting to set Sarah's teeth on edge by the second course. He had spoken when he had to speak but not otherwise.

'The coffee will be served in the drawing-room,' he informed her finally, flinging down his linen napkin.

Sarah had been too tense to eat much. Their surroundings impressed her to death: the rich décor, the gleaming period furniture, the fresh flower arrangements and the exquisite dinner service, not to mention the servants. She preceded Alex into the drawing-room and found herself gaping at a Canaletto above the marble fireplace with helpless fascination and an increasing feeling of being badly out of her depth.

The maid poured coffee. As soon as the door closed behind her, Alex murmured, 'Let's get down to business. I will naturally expect you to sign a pre-nuptial contract. I have already instructed my lawyers to draw one up.'

Was she prepared to marry him? It would not be a normal marriage. It would be a business arrangement for Nicky's benefit. Her nephew's rights of inheritance and his welfare would be secured. Nicky would have her...and she would have Nicky, she realised with a flood of warmth and relief. It wouldn't matter if Alex spent most of his time flying round the globe...in fact it would be a bonus, she decided. Why shouldn't she marry him? Callie would certainly have wanted her son to have the very best, and in this one way Sarah could ensure that

that was exactly what Nicky received. Not just the material advantages but the love and support that were equally important.

What did she have to lose? Her freedom ... What freedom would she have anyway with a young child? It was not as though she had any desire for a man in her life. Alex would continue to visit Athens and Paris and Sarah would carve out her own existence round Nicky. The only real difference would be that, for the very first time that she could remember, she would have no financial worries.

'I will not marry you without the contract.'

'No problem,' Sarah murmured, not even looking at him, quite unconcerned by what clearly most preoccupied him. His filthy lucre. And the conservation of it.

'I'll send someone over with any forms that need to be filled in and you'll be informed of the wedding arrangements in due course. Do you have any questions?'

'Why have you agreed to this?'

'For the child's sake.' Hooded dark eyes with the merest glimmer of gold rested on her, and an odd little shiver ran down her backbone. 'I want him to have what he needs most: security, love and a peaceful home.'

Why was it that she wasn't convinced? Why was it that some sixth sense sought to warn her that he was not telling her the truth? She suppressed her uneasiness irritably. He could gain nothing else but Nicky from a marriage empty of love, desire and even liking. And then the bitterness surged up inside her, blurring the clarity of her thoughts.

It should have been Callie and Damon. Her fingers tightened round her fine porcelain cup. She wanted Alex Terzakis to pay for hurting and humiliating Callie and for denying her the man she loved. Her stomach knotted up sickly. Yes, he deserved to pay ... and pay he would, if she had anything to do with it!

'You don't appear to have very much to say to me,' he noted softly.

'I've got what I wanted.' Sarah threw him a malicious smile.

He might have been carved from marble. Not a muscle moved on his strikingly hard features. He would make a terrific poker player, she conceded. He had to be hiding his rage. His fierce pride would force him to conceal his fury at being forced into marriage with a woman he despised. And she wanted to humble that macho pride just as he had once humbled Callie.

'You seem very sure of that,' Alex commented with a curiously slumbrous look in his dark eyes as they rested on her delicate profile.

'I am.' A sense of triumphant righteousness was filling her to capacity. There *was* justice in the world, after all. Alex Terzakis was not untouchable. She had him right where she wanted him ... in the palm of her hand.

'Well, what do you think?' Ruefully conscious of Gina's dropped jaw, Sarah cast aside her load of shopping-bags and pirouetted in the narrow hallway. 'Does it suit me?'

'Your hair ...' Gina whispered dazedly, taking in the silver-blonde mane now frothing over Sarah's shoulders in a torrent of silky waves. 'You've had it cut and styled ... and that suit, those shoes ...' In frank astonishment, the older woman stared at the beautifully cut mauve jacket and skirt lovingly hugging Sarah's slender figure. 'You look like a million dollars. I could have walked past you in the street without recognising you!'

'Good.' Sarah started upstairs.

'Do you really think you ought to be spending Alex's money before you marry him?' Gina murmured uneasily.

'I love spending Alex's money,' Sarah confided truthfully. 'He thinks I'm greedy and grasping. That contract made that clear enough. Twenty pages of insults. I think I ought to satisfy his expectations, don't you?'

'Has it occurred to you that you'll still have to live with the man?'

'I haven't the slightest intention of *living* with him,' Sarah asserted. 'I dare say I'll see him at the occasional mealtime...but, the way we feel about each other, I should imagine our meetings will be few and far between.'

'Then why this staggering transformation?'

Sarah dealt her an outraged look and then laughed. 'Gina, this isn't for his benefit...it's for Nicky's.'

'*Nicky's*?'

'I have to look the part to be his mother, don't I? I have to *fit*,' Sarah stressed with serious emphasis. 'Otherwise, I'll embarrass him in a few years' time. Anyway, I've only done what Alex suggested. Put myself in the hands of the professionals so that I can look reasonably presentable...'

Gina swallowed hard. Sarah looked more than reasonably presentable, she looked luminously beautiful, and her small stature, no longer dwarfed by unflattering clothing, now revealed the fragile delicacy of her slender curves. But nobody knew better than Gina that any such assurance would be greeted by hurt rejection. Sarah had spent far too many years thinking of herself as plain to be easily convinced that she had in fact chosen to make herself look plain.

Not remotely like a prison wardress, Sarah reflected as she studied her appearance in the bedroom mirror. Money could buy the illusion of beauty. *His* money. After reading that grossly insulting pre-nuptial contract, Sarah had been furious. In the first place, it had initially been presented to her in Greek. She had had to demand an English translation before she'd finally condescended to sign the Greek version in several places. In reward for her apparent docility, she had then been handed several credit cards and informed that accounts had been opened in her name.

'It's not too late to change your mind, admit you had a brainstorm and that you really didn't mean it,' Gina sighed from the doorway.

Sarah groaned. Gina hadn't once let up on the argument over the past week. 'I haven't had any second thoughts,' she admitted. 'I'm doing this for Nicky.'

'But you're not too unhappy that it demands a considerable sacrifice from Alex Terzakis?'

Emerald eyes fired. 'What do you think?'

'I think he isn't a male *I* would like to cross. I think you're crazy and, if anything, he's even more crazy to have agreed . . .'

'So tell me,' Alex murmured tautly, 'how did you do it?'

Do what? Sarah threw an uneasy glance at the male seated beside her in the limousine. She was as physically far away from him as she could get but somehow it still didn't feel far enough. He was making her feel grossly uncomfortable. This was the first time Alex had actually spoken since the ceremony in the register office.

Mind you, he had more than made up for his silence by staring, she conceded irritably. If it had been any other man, she would have said that her improved appearance had literally struck him dumb but Sarah could not credit that some new clothes, a rather silly hairstyle and a few cosmetics could genuinely dredge such a staggered response from a male reputed to be a connoisseur of the world's beautiful women. She suspected that he was attempting to send her up cruelly for her, no doubt in his eyes, pathetic efforts to measure up to her new status as Nicky's mother.

'Do what?' Her arms felt empty without Nicky. Ignoring her new husband, Sarah cast a nakedly anxious glance back at the car following them. It contained Nicky . . . and a nanny. A *real* nanny in a uniform, and no Mary Poppins either in Sarah's opinion.

When Nicky had screeched blue murder at being insensitively thrust by Alex into the strange woman's arms, the nanny had tightened her mouth and said archly, 'I can see you're a spoiled little boy,' and Sarah had rather suspected that Nanny Brown meant it. She wondered if this was the right moment to tell Alex that she did not want a nanny for Nicky and that she intended to devote herself personally to his full-time care.

'How did you achieve this astonishing metamorphosis virtually overnight?' Alex demanded in a low growl.

Sarah flushed, convinced that he was being hatefully sarcastic. She tilted her chin. 'I hired an image consultant.'

'I beg your pardon?' Alex sounded almost dazed.

'When you don't know how to do something, you consult a higher authority.'

'And what didn't you know how to do?'

Her ripe mouth, expertly enriched by lipstick the exact shade of her peach-coloured shoes, tightened and then she noticed that his dark gaze seemed to be positively welded to her lips and instinctively withdrew even further into her self-imposed corner. What on earth was the matter with him? Why was he asking such stupid questions? After all, it had been he who had given her the idea in the first place. 'With concentrated effort and professional advice, you could be quite attractive . . .' he had said, buttering her up, of course.

'I didn't know how to make the best of myself with clothes and that sort of stuff. Frankly, I never had the time or the interest before,' she muttered defensively. 'Or the money to do it.'

'You spent a pittance.'

He couldn't be serious. She had spent a *fortune* on her own terms. Admittedly, her new wardrobe didn't include any designer labels but it did include classic separates and suits that would not date and a rainbow collection of shoes, handbags and lingerie. And the consultant, whose advice had been indispensable, had cost an arm and a leg!

'An absolute pittance,' Alex repeated, continuing to scan her elegance with narrowed eyes.

He really meant it, she registered. Virtue one. Alex Terzakis was not stingy.

'And I am flattered that you were moved to such effort upon my behalf.'

'Your behalf?' Sarah echoed blankly. Dear heaven, for flattered read smug and amused...the conceited swine! she thought. 'I did this for Nicky. Why on earth would I do it for you?'

'Nicky?' he repeated very drily.

'I don't want to embarrass him——'

'He's six weeks old!' Alex suddenly raked at her incredulously.

'I don't ever want to be a mother that he will be ashamed of,' Sarah responded shortly.

'And what about gracing me with a wife that I don't have to be ashamed of?'

Sarah regarded him with blatant astonishment, without even trying making it painfully obvious that such an ambition would never have occurred to her in a million years.

A dark flush had highlighted Alex's savagely high cheekbones. He was outraged, she realised. Dear heaven, were all male egos this fragile? This was a marriage of convenience and he loathed her not one whit less than she loathed him. Why would she want to make herself more attractive for *his* benefit?

'I wish you would stop staring at me,' she muttered tightly, accusingly.

'What did you expect?' he drawled flatly. 'You have altered yourself out of all recognition...apart from the hair...'

His accented voice had dropped in pitch and disturbingly roughened. Involuntarily, Sarah felt her every

muscle tighten. Like a mesmerised statue, she watched
a lean brown hand reach out across the great divide that
separated them and flick one long shining silver strand
and then linger.

Her heart in her mouth, her shocked eyes helplessly
glued to smouldering gold ones, Sarah jerked back like
a bristling cat cornered by a pit bull terrier, plastering
her slender body against the door behind her.

'Stop that,' Alex intoned in a growl of terrifying threat,
a ferocious anger simmering in his intent gaze and
hardened face.

'Stop wh-what?' Sarah stared down with horrified eyes
at the beautifully shaped brown fingers winding, for
some peculiar reason, into a whole hank of her tumbling
mane of hair. He was imprisoning her. She absolutely
couldn't breathe and she was trembling, her body
seeming to have found a movement of its own in response to the terrible tension that had come out of
nowhere.

She didn't know what he was doing! Was he a violent
man? Was he planning to hit her or something? In a
frantic attempt to distract him, she gasped, 'I don't want
Nicky to have a nanny.'

Lush ebony lashes swept up. For a long and timeless
instant, brilliant golden eyes probed hers in stark, incredulous frustration. 'A nanny?' he almost whispered,
as though she had spoken in some strange foreign
language.

Her taut mouth wobbled. 'I'll look after him.'

'You will be far too busy looking after me,' Alex
countered in a black velvet purr.

'You have servants to do that.'

'No, I have a wife now to do that.' Alex had shifted
right across the back seat and she really was cornered
now. His other hand came up and pushed up her chin,
forcing the eye contact that she sought to avoid in
her confusion.

Throwing him a look of infuriated bemusement, Sarah brought up both hands and planted them on his broad chest to hold him at bay. Suddenly he laughed with a raw spontaneity that shook her.

'Get your hands off me...*now*!' Sarah demanded imperiously, maddened by his inexplicable behaviour.

'Make me,' Alex Terzakis invited with devastating effect.

Shimmering green eyes met savage gold ones and the shock to her system was electrifying. An utterly merciless amusement had slashed his hard mouth into a vibrant smile. Her mouth ran dry. Beneath her now frantically spread hands she could feel the heat of his powerful body and the steady thump of his heartbeat. Her own heartbeat was racing like an express train, something akin to panic threatening to rip asunder her once icy composure. And more intimately still the scent of him was in her nostrils, all male laced with some faintly spicy cologne that was disturbingly erotic. Erotic? Dear lord, where had that thought come from?

Disorientatingly, he vented another soft laugh and slid gracefully back from her, his every movement fluid and smooth and confident. He was a male very much at home with his own physical presence. Hooded dark eyes surveyed her with unreadable cool and something else— something else she could not quite put a name to but which might have been satisfaction.

'Thank you,' she said in an arctic tone, skimming not quite steady hands down over her jacket as though he might have crumpled it by daring to come that close.

'That ring on your finger is a wedding-ring,' Alex intoned softly.

Sarah's classically perfect nose wrinkled as she cast a throwaway glance at the item. 'So?' she said drily.

'You are now my wife.'

Her emerald eyes glinted. *His wife*. Was she expected to cower in terror or preen herself with pride? The wedding had meant nothing to her. It had been an empty ceremony, as meaningless now that it was over as the platinum band on her finger. Their marriage had satisfied two needs: Sarah's desire to have the right to oversee Nicky's future and Sarah's desire for revenge. She had made Alex Terzakis pay for destroying her sister's happiness. She had forced him to marry her. But, now that that was achieved, the furious fire of her fevered bitterness had begun to ebb. He had paid the price that she'd demanded and she really had nothing more to say to Alex Terzakis. Ahead of her stretched a new life with the baby she loved. Alex Terzakis would merely stand on the sidelines of that life, his sole role being that of playing occasional father to the best of his ability. They had nothing to talk about, nothing in common, nothing to share beyond Nicky. So why the macho stress on the concept that she was *his wife*? The term was irrelevant.

'You are so punch-drunk on your triumph that you have developed tunnel vision,' Alex asserted smoothly.

In exasperation, Sarah tossed her hair back. The shining mass flowed down her back in a tumbling river of silver. Big hair, she thought, like someone out of a glitzy novel. She wished she had had it cut short. She didn't like the way Alex's eyes lingered on it. It seemed to attract his attention and she didn't feel comfortable with that.

'I do not like being ignored.'

'Perhaps you should try making normal conversation if you *have* to speak,' Sarah returned, fed up with his mysterious remarks that seemed calculated to try and stir up her misgivings.

'About the weather? That would be just about your level.'

'The rain in Spain fell mainly on the plain,' she enunciated sweetly.

'What age are you?'

'Why don't you look at your marriage licence?'

'Don't be childish.'

'In a month's time, I will be twenty-five ... I still have a year or two left before I hit thirty,' Sarah could not resist stressing.

'That hurt, did it?'

'Nothing you could say or do could hurt me. Where you are concerned, I am inviolable,' Sarah stated with conviction.

'You are very confident.'

'I have reason to be.' Sarah had thought it all out.

What *could* he do to her? He could keep her short of money. It wouldn't bother her. He could ignore her. It would please her. He could be rude. She would answer him back. He could disport himself in a different woman's bed every night, flaunt his promiscuity to society at large ... it wouldn't disturb her, except in so far as he would not be setting much of an example for Nicky to follow in later years. And if he was violent she would divorce him ... or she would divorce what was left of him by the time she had finished with him. One hint of physical abuse, she reflected fierily, and he was a male with a severely limited lifespan!

They boarded the jet which was to take them to Alex's home in France. Sarah hovered, ignoring the proffered seat. As Nanny Brown climbed the steps, Sarah heard Nicky's screams and raced forward, pale and stricken.

'It's quite all right, madam,' the older woman forestalled her with a determined little smile. 'Nikos and I do require some time to become acquainted. I've been looking after children for thirty years and he'll soon get used to me.'

'Perhaps in small doses. He's scared of strangers.' Sarah held out her arms.

'Maybe he's not well.' Alex had moved forward. His dark, powerful face was troubled as he gazed down at his screeching nephew.

'There's nothing the matter with him but bad temper,' Nanny asserted. 'Babies have to accustom themselves to a routine.'

Tears smarting behind her worried eyes, Sarah couldn't stand it any longer. She reached out and simply took Nicky, cuddling him close, muttering baby talk as she hurriedly moved back down the aisle. Nicky unglued swollen dark eyes and looked up at her, his mouth alarmingly enlarged on the brink of another howl. He thought better of it and nestled his damp head into her cradling hand.

Sarah took her seat with contentment. Alex studied them both with narrowed eyes. 'He knows you...'

'Of course he does... don't you, my darling?' Her small hand stroked the baby's head in just the way he liked to be soothed and quieted. Glancing up, she found herself in receipt of an intense and frowning appraisal and she wondered why Alex should look at her like that, as if she were behaving strangely. Whether he liked it or not, she was fulfilling the role she was here for and unless the nanny he had arrogantly engaged without consultation betrayed a softer, more flexible attitude Sarah had no intention of leaving Nicky in her care.

She fed Nicky while Nanny glowered disapproval from the other end of the spacious cabin.

'Are you trying to impress me at this late date?' Alex enquired with crushing contempt.

Sarah blinked. 'What on earth are you talking about?'

'All this mock-maternal attention for Nikos?' he derided. 'Why do you think I engaged a nanny?'

'There is nothing mock about my feelings for my nephew,' Sarah countered with a disdain and a temper only controlled by the presence of the baby in her arms. She had no intention of fighting with Alex when Nicky was within hearing distance. A baby could be upset by raised, sharp voices and tension. 'And I would sooner not comment on your acquisition of a nanny...although

I could say that I'm not too impressed by what I've seen so far.'

'She comes with the highest references.'

Sarah's sultry mouth tautened. 'I don't want to be prematurely critical or unfair, but you did about as well as I would have expected, interfering in something about which you know nothing ... something I imagine you do with monotonous regularity,' she could not resist stabbing, 'because you are one of those men who always think they know *everything*——'

His lower lip had briefly parted company with the upper. A splintering tension screamed from his stillness. He could not believe what he was hearing. A home truth or two and he was ready to explode. Certainly not a product of an upbringing by any Nanny Brown, she thought with sudden helpless amusement. This was a male so absolutely unaccustomed to even the smallest censure that his first response was anger and outrage. Probably spoilt rotten as a child. Born rich, clever, very good-looking. Ambitious, successful, workaholic and domineering, doubtless encouraged by an adoring family and grovelling employees and fawning, stupid women to believe himself the very zenith of perfection in every field. Medallion man with brains, no less.

'Are you a lesbian?'

After a staggered pause, a rosy flush swept up the pale skin of her throat. Sarah stared back at him incredulously. And then abruptly, surprising herself, she laughed out loud. That ego of his ... He just could not accept that she should be unimpressed and unattracted by him.

'I thought not.' Far from being ill at ease, Alex trained his night-dark gaze upon her with glittering intensity, a faint but definable smile of grim amusement curving his handsome mouth. 'Then ask yourself why you feel such a powerful compulsion to try and put me down.'

Sarah opened her jewel-like eyes very wide with pretended naïveté. 'Do I really? And you mean you actually noticed?' she gasped.

In a silence of the utmost self-assurance, Alex surveyed her with the lazy indolence of a jungle predator, and, since she found that impregnable cool disturbing, she went on, 'You see, I don't like you, Alex——'

'Liking isn't required . . . but I will have respect.'

There was a sizzle in the atmosphere. Sarah revelled in it. 'It's good for a man to have a goal to work towards . . . even when the goal will remain eternally out of reach.'

'You tread where even my most powerful enemies dare not tread.'

The assurance hung there and provoked an insidious chill down her rigid backbone. Under the drugging onslaught of icy dark eyes, she denied that weakness within her. 'I am not afraid of you.'

Alex's lushly framed gaze dropped to the slender hand unwittingly gripping the arm of her seat. 'Your body language says otherwise. If I banished Nanny and the stewardess, you'd be out of here like a hare with the hounds on its trail.'

Paling, she breathed, 'What an intriguing image that would be and it tells me so much about you. If you can't reduce a woman to grovelling admiration, you'd settle for fear . . . in fact, you'd settle for just about anything sooner than deal with a woman on any other level——'

'A woman like you . . . yes,' Alex intoned with a low, vicious bite that slashed through her taught nerve-endings like a machete. 'This is not how I foresaw my wedding-day.'

Sarah stiffened, an idea that had never before occurred to her occurring to her now. 'How had you foreseen it?'

'That I would share it with a bride worthy of my name.'

'And you said you weren't a snob...'

'It is not your background which disturbs me but your lack of morality.'

'*My* lack of morality?'

'The woman whom I would have married has the very highest principles.'

And there it was, what she had never thought of, never dreamt of, never even considered for the smallest moment. 'Are you saying that you were engaged to someone?' she whispered tremulously, completely appalled by the idea.

'I was contemplating matrimony.'

'Did you love her?' Sarah was trembling, plunged into genuine distress.

'I have no intention of discussing my private life with you——'

'Did she love you? Dear lord, why didn't you tell me?' Sarah demanded.

Alex stretched out long, powerful legs and tossed back a whisky in one driven gesture.

'You have no right to lay this on me when you never even mentioned that there might be someone in your life...I mean someone apart from——'

'The women I have to *pay* to share my bed?' Alex slotted in dulcetly.

From pale Sarah turned crimson, unprepared to have that thrown up to her when she was in such turmoil. The very idea that she might have broken some poor woman's heart by depriving her of the man she loved, even if it was Alex Terzakis, now sat on Sarah's conscience like a giant boulder.

'Elise never shared my bed.'

Not much of a passionate romance, then, Sarah decided.

'Nor was marriage ever broached as a subject between us, but we would eventually have made a suitable alliance. In the Terzakis family, we marry for life. One does not enter such a serious commitment in a romantic haze of illusion.'

'God forbid,' Sarah mumbled, thinking how coldly calculating he was. Sex with his mistresses. Stability and suitability with his wife. Love just didn't come into the equation. And why should she be surprised? Callie had been judged and rejected on those same terms. Sarah had no doubt that Damon's bride Androula was rich, well-born and suitable in the extreme.

Yet Sarah *was* surprised by Alex's matrimonial equation. Strive as he might to conceal the fact, Alex emanated emotional and passionate intensity in perceptible waves. His responses ran deep and strong and he was immensely protective of his family, whether she liked his methods or not. He had divided Damon from Callie because he'd believed that to be in his kid brother's best interests and had doubtless married him off fast to ensure that there were no further *unsuitable* alliances.

'Does Elise love you?'

Alex elevated a superior winged brow at the intimacy of the question.

Sarah flushed but refused to be silenced. 'I would hate to think that I had been the cause of hurting her.'

'I hurt her pride,' Alex divulged grimly. 'And since she and everyone else will believe that Nicky is *my* child and *you* are his mother...'

Sarah frowned. 'Must they?'

'Something else you didn't consider?' Alex derided. 'Since Damon and Androula are not to have the right to raise Nicky as their child, his true parentage must remain a secret within the family circle. I will not have Androula humiliated...'

Sarah didn't see how Androula could be humiliated by something that had occurred before her marriage to

Damon…unless Androula had been on scene at the same time as Callie. That was possible, she supposed. Damon had betrayed his true character in his treatment of Callie. Androula could well have been the socially acceptable girl back home in Greece.

'Naturally, as soon as Nicky is of an age to understand, he will be told that he is adopted and, later still, I believe that he should have every right to know the whole truth of his parentage——'

'Your whole truth or mine?'

Alex dealt her a slashing look of sudden intimidation. 'You are a malicious and very dangerous woman, but be warned…I will tolerate no interference on that count when the time comes. If you're still around, of course.'

The soft conclusion made her tense. 'Why wouldn't I be around?' she asked stiffly.

'You will require remarkable staying power and buckets of humility to stay the course,' Alex drawled, his dark, strong face set in unyielding lines, a rather dauntingly amused smile playing round the edges of his hard mouth. 'And frankly I do not think you are likely to make the grade.'

'Thank you for the vote of confidence.'

But Sarah was suffering from increasing turmoil. He was threatening her but that alone would not have plunged her into her current slough of self-examination. What threatened her most of all was her very first acknowledgement of Alex as a male with feelings and possible frailties of his own.

He was very bitter. Three weeks ago, she hadn't given two hoots for that, would have felt equal to holding off Alex with one hand and an army with the other. Grieving for Callie, distraught with bitterness and fiercely driven by her own need for revenge, Sarah had closed her eyes to one inescapably basic reality. Damon was the male who had lied to Callie, got her pregnant, abandoned her, neglected to support her and furthermore lied about her to his brother. Acting on information received, Alex had moved into action. Damon could have gone ahead and married Callie, defying his brother, if he had wanted to. But the simple truth was that Damon hadn't wanted to marry Callie and indeed had scarpered, leaving Alex to extract him from an embarrassing situation.

So Damon was the real sinner but Alex was the one making the sacrifices. Dear God, how come that was only penetrating her confused brain *now*? Why had the entirety of her hatred focused solely on Alex Terzakis? He had been a far more worthy opponent on which to target her rage than his wimpy little brother, who had been assiduously careful to put in only the most fleeting appearance at Callie's funeral. Yet she had forced Alex to make restitution on Damon's behalf.

Sarah felt suddenly like someone emerging into the sunlight after a long period of being lost somewhere underground. 'It's not too late to change your mind, admit you had a brainstorm and that you really didn't mean it,' Gina had urged over and over again before the wedding. But Sarah had been deaf and blind to such persuasions. She had had a Terzakis male in her sights and she had taken aim and fired in the name of revenge.

And for Nicky, she reminded herself. And for Nicky. Unfortunately, it was only now registering that she had just about wrecked Alex's life while Damon got off scot-free and that was not justice. From below her fluttering lashes, she appraised the husband she had acquired by force, collided electrifyingly with fierce golden eyes as hot as flames and hurriedly dropped her gaze again, a dismaying sinking sensation afflicting her stomach. Bloody hell, girl, she said to herself furiously, this is not the time to lose your bottle!

CHAPTER FIVE

A CHÂTEAU in the Loire Valley...what else for a
Terzakis? Sarah asked herself as the limousine wafted
them at a stately pace down an avenue girded on both
sides by a marching procession of huge lime trees, their
graceful, pendent foliage shimmering as the light breeze
played with the leaves.

'How long have you lived here?' Sarah was entranced
enough to speak freely as a resplendent building,
fashioned of pale creamy stone and built in the classical
tradition, began to come into view at the foot of the
avenue. 'Gosh...it's huge!' she gasped when she be-
latedly absorbed the two wings curving back in sym-
metrical style from the three-storey-high central block.

'This was my mother's family home.'

'She was French? When did she die?' Sarah asked,
suddenly thirsty for information.

'When I was a child,' Alex retorted in a quelling tone
that suggested she was trespassing on forbidden territory.

Sarah bent her head, suddenly embarrassed by her own
adolescent excitement. But she had never been abroad
in her life before, hadn't even crossed the Channel on a
day trip to Calais. It was very difficult to take her abrupt
change in circumstances coolly in her stride when she
was faced with a fabulous château looking like something out of a fairy-tale.

Without warning, Alex leant forward to stare out incredulously at the female figure surging out of the palatial main entrance towards their car as it drew to a
halt. He ground out a stifled imprecation in his own
language and then groaned out loud. Momentarily, be-

79

neath Sarah's astounded gaze, he looked like a male waiting for an express train to drive over him—helpless.

'If you dare to betray by even a hint that Nicky is not our child, I will kill you,' Alex hissed half under his breath.

And the way he looked at her, Sarah believed him. 'But who is——?'

She got no further. The chauffeur opened the car door. The small blonde woman, waiting impatiently, enveloped her straight into an enthusiastic and affectionate embrace.

'I'm your mother-in-law,' she said cheerfully.

'Sarah, this is Vivien, my stepmother——'

'Always so precise when anybody could tell you that I've loved him like my own for over twenty years,' Vivien sighed.

'You're English,' was all Sarah could find to say weakly, feeling engulfed.

'Alex, I know I'm more than a little out of order just landing like this on your wedding night,' Vivien was appealing with pleading eyes while Alex stood there towering over her like a monolith carved out of stone. 'But you do see that I simply couldn't wait to meet Sarah, who is going to make you astonishingly happy... and how can I tell that before I get to know her? She hugged me back. Pounced on by a total stranger and she hugged me back because she didn't want to hurt my feelings!'

'Vivien,' Alex attempted to insert a word into the endless flood.

'No hug?' Vivien looked expectant.

Alex bent down to peck the proffered cheek.

'I see he still counts you as an audience, Sarah. He's usually a little more enthusiastic... Well, where is he?'

'Who?' Alex breathed.

'Alex, what's the matter with you? Your *son*. I am just dying to get my hands on him!'

The other car drew up. Nanny emerged, complete with Nicky. Vivien surged over and then slowly retreated a step.

'Let us go into the house. I will have you shown to your room.' Alex anchored a hand like a vice to Sarah's elbow, dragging her in his wake, evidently keen to remove her from his charming stepmother's radius.

But Vivien cut them off. 'Nanny says he's asleep and mustn't be disturbed,' she stage-whispered with a grimace. 'Bit of a dragon, isn't she? Your choice, Alex?'

'Yes,' Sarah confirmed.

'Your son is *gorgeous*, Sarah.' Vivien patted her arm warmly. 'You are a clever girl, and so slim again so quickly. Looking at you, nobody would ever dream you're a very new mother. Are you breast-feeding?'

Sarah reddened fiercely. 'No.'

'I'll take Nikos up to the nursery, madam.' Nanny sailed past.

'She's like a tank, isn't she?' Vivien remarked. 'I can see her putting up barricades to keep us out.'

Sarah giggled. 'Can't you just?'

'Alex, I am not going to stay...I promise you. I won't even be staying to dinner. I'm flying straight back home again as soon as I leave. But really, Alex,' Vivien lamented, leading them into the château, 'it's all your own fault. That ghastly hole and corner wedding you subjected this darling girl to today! No friends, no family, no reception...not even a honeymoon—shabby. I could have done it in style. I do want you to know that I *pleaded* with him, Sarah. Even with only three weeks to play with, I could have made it the wedding of the year.'

A line of staff was assembled in the vast entrance hall. 'I know, positively medieval, isn't it?' Vivien whispered sympathetically, reading Sarah's dismay.

Alex performed the introductions, but all formality was swiftly banished by Vivien, who also concluded the interlude by linking her arm with Sarah's, saying, 'Now

I expect you'd like to freshen up,' and carrying Sarah
with determination towards the grand stone staircase.

'Bit of an atmosphere between you two, isn't there?'
Vivien commented with a sigh. 'I adore Alex but it does
take two to tango, doesn't it? And it happens even in
the best of families. And who could call such a gorgeous
baby an accident? Frankly, I'd call him a miracle...Alex
saved at the eleventh hour from deep-freezing himself
into eternity with that dreadful Elise—you do know
about her, don't you?'

'A little.'

'A little's more than enough. She's the most fright-
fully perfect woman. Speaks several languages, is an ac-
complished artist, owns one of the most famous
vineyards in the Loire and can trace her family tree back
for yonks and yonks. Incredibly beautiful too. But she's
very superior—treats me like the proverbial dumb
blonde, which I'm not...and she would have undone
all the hard work I put into unfreezing Alex. Elise doesn't
have any emotions. I think she had them vacuumed out
in a special operation so that she could function more
like a robot!'

'But she must have been hurt...'

'Not at all. She doesn't love Alex any more than he
loved her. They were going to get together some day and
hatch a dynasty, probably in a test tube...I really couldn't
imagine her doing it the normal way. She might get her
hair mussed. Thank God your birth control let you
down!' Vivien asserted. 'You saved Alex from a fate
worse than death!'

Vivien's constant chatter allowed Sarah to picture
exactly what the older woman had been told. Alex had
admitted he was making a shotgun wedding, purely for
the sake of legitimising his child, it seemed. At least there
was no need to put up a front of being a joyous and
adored bride.

Vivien pressed her into a huge and opulent bedroom, festooned with white flowers everywhere she looked. 'Got it all ready for you behind his back,' she confided.

Sarah focused on the colossal carved oak four-poster. It was also hung with masses of fresh flowers, resembling some fantastic scene from a film, she thought, on the edge of hysteria. She could barely breathe for the heaviness of the perfume in the air.

'It's beautiful,' she mumbled as Vivien regarded her. 'Stunning,' she added weakly.

'Alex said I wouldn't like you. I was terrified,' Vivien admitted. 'I mean, someone worse than Elise after all the plotting and planning I've been doing to keep her at bay! And Alex acting like he had been trapped... It would take an Amazon to trap Alex!'

The Amazon moistened her dry lips. 'It wasn't a trap but I did employ pressure,' Sarah heard herself saying, desperately wanting to be as honest as possible.

'You had to do that?' Vivien's pretty, animated face looked astonished. 'With Alex? The *rat*!' she exclaimed. 'I always thought Alex could be depended on one hundred per cent to do the decent thing——'

'Oh, he can be——' Sarah backtracked hastily.

'He has a very strong sense of honour and responsibility. Makes him a bit pious sometimes.' Vivien pulled a face. 'But he adores children.'

'Yes.'

'Got rather rigid ideas, though. I spoilt Damon—that's Alex's younger brother—dreadfully. He was such a charmer when he was a boy... not that I don't still love him but he does worry me sometimes.' Vivien leant back against the massive footboard of the bed, looking abstracted and troubled. 'You know, you'll laugh, but when I first heard there was a baby I actually thought Alex might be trying to cover for Damon.'

Sarah had frozen. 'Oh?' was all she was capable of saying.

'And it would totally have broken Andy's heart, and she had been looking a bit peaky and strained lately. Worships the ground Damon walks on——'

'Andy?'

'My daughter, Androula.'

'Your daughter is married to Alex's brother?'

'I was a widow with a little girl when I met Alex's father,' Vivien explained, with a far-away look in her eyes. 'My first husband was also Greek. I worked in Nikos's office. I couldn't take dictation for tacks but he was always asking for me! Not that he had honourable intentions, let me tell you. Nikos had me earmarked as his next pillow-friend——'

'His what?' Still reeling from the shock that Damon's wife was this woman's daughter, doubly a part of the Terzakis family because she must have grown up with both brothers as a stepsister, Sarah was none the less fascinated by Vivien's story.

'A little Greek euphemism for mistress.' Vivien wrinkled her nose. 'I said no and no and no again for an entire year and always kept a desk between us. At the end of it he was on his knees begging me to marry him but hating me too, if you know what I mean. So we married and it took me another two years to get rid of what you might call the baggage from his previous life-style——'

'Baggage?'

'The mistress he did have. He just couldn't understand why he couldn't have us both.' Vivien fixed bright blue eyes ruefully on Sarah. 'I presume you are aware that Alex keeps his left luggage in Athens and Paris?'

'Er...yes.'

'Greek men have double standards,' Vivien muttered with rich sympathy. 'Want to know how I kicked out the baggage?'

'Love to,' Sarah said truthfully.

'I made him jealous. A dangerous game, that, but for me, it worked. All of a sudden he realised how *I* felt and he never strayed again, he was so busy watching my every move. I loved him to death but boy, did I keep him on his toes. What are your plans?'

'Plans?'

'You need a strategy if you want to decimate the opposition. Remember, I'm always at the end of the phone and I come to Paris all the time. I'll be here in a fortnight again to see my grandson properly.' Vivien was already drifting to the door. She turned back for a second and smiled. 'Alex has a conscience . . . play on it . . . and of course *that*.' She indicated the bed meaningfully beneath Sarah's embarrassed gaze. 'I'm sure you're already quite aware that what happens in here is more important than anything else right now. Don't let the sun go down on a row . . .'

Sarah nodded dumbly in receipt of her instructions.

'See you next week.' The door shut on Vivien.

Sarah collapsed down on a chair, feeling as though she had tangled with a whirlwind. She was beginning to understand why Alex had looked momentarily helpless. Vivien was a miniature dynamo. And the poor woman was actually rooting for this crazy marriage to work because evidently Sarah was viewed as a lesser evil than Elise!

But Vivien was the mother of Damon's wife. That opened up whole new areas of conjecture. Talk about keeping it in the family! Slowly Sarah shook her buzzing head. The extent of her own ignorance was colossal and frustrating. She knew nothing about the Terzakis family that Callie had not chosen to tell her and she had not seen Alex once in the three weeks which had come between his agreement to marry her and the actual ceremony today. No wonder Alex had been shaken by the sight of his stepmother's descent! Naturally he did not trust Sarah, who had been so vitriolic with him, to keep her mouth shut with Vivien.

Androula...'looking a bit peaky and strained,' according to her mother. Sarah broke out in a cold sweat of discomfiture. Dear God, she had been so wilfully blind in refusing to see the view from the other side of the fence! Sarah had been outraged when she'd realised that Damon had gaily married another woman while Callie was carrying his child—it had been the final insult in Sarah's book! She had regarded Androula as her sister's triumphant rival.

But how triumphant could a newish bride be, faced with the knowledge that another woman was having her husband's child and then ultimately being presented with the demand that she take on that same child and bring it up as her own? Sarah wasn't a bit surprised that Vivien's daughter was looking strained. After all, at what point had Androula learnt of Callie's condition? *Before* or *after* the wedding?

Sarah groaned out loud. Suddenly she was being forced to face yet again that there was another side to the coin of her own bitterness. Clearly Androula was suffering too and she was an entirely innocent party. Damon, she reflected grimly, spread misery wherever he went, it seemed.

Her luggage was brought up by a manservant and then a maid arrived to tell her that dinner would be served in an hour. The maid stayed to unpack. Sarah hovered, uneasy at being waited on for the very first time in her life, and in the end took refuge in the *en-suite* bathroom to freshen up and change for dinner. That achieved, she employed her schoolgirl French to the task of asking directions to the nursery.

Nanny had put up the barricades all right. Nicky was tucked into a great brass cot, fed, changed and put down for the night. 'He's settled ... finally,' the older woman stressed before Sarah could cross the threshold of the room.

'Great...'

'It wouldn't be a good idea to disturb him.'

Gritting her teeth, Sarah withdrew again. If she disturbed her nephew and he started to cry, she would be leaving Nanny to cope while she went down to dinner.

'And I'll be retiring now, Mrs Terzakis. I'm very tired.'

'I'll see to his night feeds,' Sarah said cheerfully.

Nanny looked at her in amazement. 'Not at all, madam. There is no necessity for that. I'll manage tonight and tomorrow, I believe, some help will be arriving—a young girl to step in for the late feeds and cover for my time off.'

Glory be. Nicky was going to be under twenty-four-hour surveillance! Sarah went downstairs at speed, her wide green eyes furious. Nicky was being taken over by staff hired by Alex. Sarah was being replaced and made superfluous.

A hovering manservant, evidently awaiting her arrival in the hall, flung wide the door of the dining-room.

'I hate unpunctuality.'

Alex was standing by a massive fireplace, cradling a drink in one brown hand. As she took in his immaculate appearance in a tailored dinner-jacket, Sarah tensed, acknowledging her first social error. She should have put on the single evening gown she had purchased. Did he dress up *every* night to dine?

She took her seat at one end of the long, polished table, lit by an ornate set of silver candelabra, and ran an uncertain hand through her tumbling hair, intimidated, though the sensation ran strongly against her natural spirit.

'Your stepmother's very nice,' she murmured. 'Astonishingly nice actually. She made me feel very welcome.'

Alex's expressive mouth twisted sardonically. He signalled the manservant. A minute later all the candles on the table had been doused and the great chandelier above had been illuminated to shed blinding light on the vast contours of a room which had been romantically shrunken into intimacy by the candles.

'The staff may believe we have something to celebrate; I do not.'

Sarah appraised his darkly handsome features, an odd tugging pulling at the pit of her stomach and interfering with her thought processes. But his gesture of cynical rebellion against the expectations of his servants made her want to throw something at him. The staff were not to know that this was not a normal wedding night, and the exquisite flowers adorning the table made it obvious that Alex's staff, presumably encouraged by Vivien, had gone to a lot of effort.

Alex took one outraged look at the oyster starter delivered and swore only half under his breath. Oysters were supposed to be an aphrodisiac, Sarah reflected, her fine complexion wreathed by sudden colour. She wondered if Alex was thinking what she was thinking. Vivien had been very busy. Not that she *could* eat the oysters anyway. Sarah had once had a very strong allergic reaction to seafood and she hadn't touched shellfish since.

'How does it feel to be my wife?'

It was a rough demand. Startled, Sarah glanced up from her untouched plate. She was shaken by the seething quality of his glittering golden eyes. They seemed to reach down the table and threaten to go for her throat. All of a sudden she was very grateful that they were seated a ludicrous distance apart.

'How?' he prompted with lethal persistence.

'Alex…I don't feel like your wife, so don't let it worry you,' she responded with a forced laugh. 'All I want to be is the best mother I can be for Nicky. I have no intention of interfering in your life in any other way.'

'Soft words,' Alex countered with rich derision. 'You seem to have been in the process of retreat ever since you got that ring on your finger.'

'I don't know where you got that impression.'

'You told me that what I deserved was a wife who made my life a living hell. A real bitch—I believe that was your expression,' he drawled. 'But now you appear to be changing your game plan...playing the devoted mother to the best of your severely limited acting ability——'

'I wasn't acting! I love Nicky!'

'He was your passport to another world. You used him,' Alex condemned in a low growl. 'You used him to get what I denied your sister!'

'That is not true. Yes, OK, I wanted revenge but I never dreamt you'd *agree*!' Sarah protested fiercely. 'Then when you did I saw that our marriage was the best possible solution for Nicky's needs——'

'You forced yourself on me.' His striking dark features set with angry distaste. 'I did not believe that any woman could be that shameless.'

'You must have led a very sheltered life.'

'Wealth and status were your price. You sold Nicky to me.'

Aghast by the charge, Sarah plunged upright. 'How dare you accuse me of that?' she gasped.

'Not that I expected anything more from the harridan who had the effrontery to face me in my office five months ago——'

'Who are you calling a harridan?' Sarah spat with disbelief, her green eyes firing with outrage.

'Neither you nor your wretched sister gave a damn about Androula. What kind of reception did you expect from me?' Alex demanded very drily. 'Damon already had a wife and a family and you knew that from the beginning of their sordid affair!'

Her eyes were huge pools of emerald in her hectically flushed face. Slowly, painfully slowly, the pink began to drain from below her skin. 'A wife *and* a f-family... *then*?' she stammered out, her tongue feeling too clumsy to assist her speech accurately. 'You are telling me that five months ago Damon had been married long enough to have a *child*? I don't believe you!'

'This pretence of ignorance will gain you nothing,' Alex stressed with stinging contempt. Your sister met Androula and my nieces before she worked her way into my brother's bed. The babysitter... hmm? Your sister was the babysitter from hell!'

Sarah was shaking so badly she had to set her wine glass down. 'You are lying. You are making up this crazy story to desecrate my sister's memory!' she accused unsteadily. 'She could never have met your sister-in-law... she couldn't even have known she existed! Callie did not know that Damon was married and neither did I.'

'Of course you knew.'

'But Damon asked Callie to marry him. He even gave her an engagement ring!'

Alex uttered a very rude word, signifying his disbelief.

Sarah flew tempestuously upright again. 'Don't you dare use language like that in front of me!' With a trembling hand, she braced herself on the chair behind her and vehemently shook her head, a cascade of silver hair shimmering round her in a luxuriant curtain. 'I don't know what you think you're playing at with these lies.'

Alex was lounging back in his carved chair, disturbingly still, dangerously silent with his night-dark eyes trained intently upon her distressed and defensive face.

Sarah thumped the table with a clumsily coiled fist, barely able to think straight. 'There is no way, absolutely no way my sister would have knowingly become involved with another woman's husband!'

She knocked over her wine glass as she lifted her hand again. Stinging tears lashed her shocked eyes. She dashed them away with furious fingers, sending him a glimmering look of naked reproach and condemnation.

'Your sister met Androula first.'

'My sister could never have met Damon's wife! She's never been to Greece in her life!' Sarah practically sobbed, afflicted by an emotional turmoil more overwhelming than anything she had ever experienced. How dared he malign Callie's memory? Damon must have lied and lied and lied again to protect himself, heaping all the blame on to Callie. It was obscene...inexcusable.

'I have proof.'

'What proof?'

Alex uncoiled his long limbs and fluidly arose from the table to walk the length of the room, six feet three inches of self-command and complete authority. He paused at the door. 'Are you coming...or don't you think you could keep this farce up faced with the evidence?'

Sarah's teeth clenched together. She fought to get a grip on her wildly flailing emotions. 'I am not afraid of any evidence that you could produce!' she asserted.

He crossed the hall and she practically had to trot to keep up with his powerful stride. He entered a room shelved on all sides by books, a library with a large desk set in front of the windows. Then he pressed something on the carved edging of one set of shelves in the corner and Sarah's eyes widened as the shelves swung back, revealing an entrance.

'I keep the evidence in the safe,' he revealed.

Sarah smoothed her damp palms down over her skirt and held her head high. She was not afraid—*no*, she was not afraid that he could show her anything that might damage her faith in her late sister!

She waited by the edge of his desk, her stomach churning sickly with tension and the extent of her distress. Damon had been married...Damon had been married from the outset! That in itself was a severe shock. But what was even more shocking was that Alex appeared to believe that Sarah and Callie had known that fact!

Alex fanned out a selection of glossy colour photos on the highly polished surface of the desk. 'They were taken in Oxford. Androula and the children flew over to spend a few weeks with Damon.'

Sarah's eyes fell on the uppermost photo and it was as though someone had punched her in the kidneys. Callie was standing beside a dark-haired young woman and each of them held the hand of a dark-haired little girl, one toddler size, the other possibly four or five years old. Everybody was smiling like mad. Sarah felt physically sick.

A long forefinger skimmed that photo out of reach and lined up the rest. Callie featured in all of them, playing with the children in a park or some such place, and in the final one she was sitting on a swing beside Damon, each of them with a child on their lap. Finally Sarah turned her head away, shutting out the photos.

'Andy mislaid one of my nieces in a shop and your sister found her. That's how they met,' Alex divulged with raw derision. 'Andy made the mistake of taking her home to dinner...and then she babysat for them once or twice. My sister-in-law returned to Greece, leaving your sister with a clear field.'

To accept that Callie had known all along that Damon was a married man, had indeed even met his wife, been befriended by her, trusted by her and had played with their daughters...it was a shock of such resounding savagery that Sarah was utterly silenced for several long seconds, the victim of immense pain and guilt. Dear God, where had she herself gone wrong in raising Callie? Where had the voice of conscience been when Callie embarked on such an affair?

'She was only eighteen...she did love him.' Sarah wasn't talking to Alex. She was reasoning with herself, seeking a defence for the sister she loved, the sister she had believed she understood. 'And heaven knows he encouraged her. The first time I met Damon he said that he loved her and he wanted to marry her——'

'Damon denies that there was ever any discussion of marriage.'

'He's lying... Dear lord, *she* lied too!' Sarah conceded painfully. 'How long has Damon been married?'

'Since he was nineteen. Andy was eighteen. It was not my wish. Indeed I strongly advised them to wait. Damon was far too young,' Alex admitted flatly. 'But Vivien supported them and my father saw no reason to withhold his consent.'

Sarah folded her arms protectively round herself, still white as a sheet, still in shock.

'You might as well have these. Unopened, you will note.' Alex extended a bundle of letters. Callie's letters. Sarah recognised her sister's copper-plate neat handwriting on the envelopes.

'He never received them,' Sarah whispered.

'I did not believe that she was pregnant,' Alex reminded her shortly.

'*He* did! You had no right to withold those letters,' Sarah told him tremulously. 'Callie wasn't some Mata Hari who seduced him away from home and hearth! She was a teenager and he was a lot older! Whether he was married or not, Callie was also his responsibility...'

Alex dealt her a sardonic appraisal. 'I am not my brother.'

'But you interfered——'

'There were innocent children involved as well as the peace and stability of my entire family,' Alex spelt out, defending his own behaviour with neither apology nor regret. 'It has always been my opinion that it is the woman's place to say no——'

'You *hypocritical*——!' Sarah slung up at him.

'Your sister knew that Damon was married. She made her choice... and my brother made his. He went back to his wife.'

Sarah passed an unsteady hand over her throbbing temples.

'Dinner,' Alex reminded her drily from the door.

'I'm not hungry any more... I think I'll go to bed,' she mumbled.

'Alone... on our wedding night?'

Sarah's dazed eyes connected involuntarily with smouldering gold and it was as though he had jerked a string and she was a puppet. Every muscle jerked tight, every nerve-ending quivered with suicidal energy. I'm not feeling well, she thought; that's why I feel peculiar.

'I'll be up later,' Alex murmured very softly, and swung on his heel. 'I just can't wait for you to lie back and think of the greater glory of Greece.'

'I beg your pardon?'

But she was talking to an empty room.

CHAPTER SIX

SARAH lay back in the vast bed, her eyes trained rigidly on the door. He'd been joking—of course he had been joking, most probably trying to deprive her of a good night's sleep. A man had to be sexually attracted to a woman to want to make love to her. Alex was not attracted to her. That compartment in Alex's life was already filled to overflowing with willing and no doubt beautiful women. He had a lousy sense of humour. It was not as though she was his wife...not his *real* wife.

Callie... Her mind gave way to another upsetting surge of thoughts. Sarah had never been so confused, could not yet credit that this woman being torn in two by indecision and uncertainty and guilt was actually herself. Sarah had always known where she was going, always been quietly very sure of her own judgement and direction...until now, that was.

Before tonight, before Alex's revelations, Sarah had been convinced that Callie had been used and abused and brutally abandoned. But now the picture had blurred and shifted and she was no longer sure of anything. Callie had deliberately concealed the truth of her relationship with Damon and, the night she had brought Damon to meet Sarah, Callie and Damon had been united in that deception. Callie had knowingly become involved with a married man and then moved in with him while his wife was abroad. Clearly, Damon had promised to get a divorce and then, probably when the heat of the affair ebbed on his side, he had changed his mind. Had her sister at that point allowed herself to become pregnant

95

in an attempt to force the issue to the conclusion she desired?

Sarah attempted to envisage her sister without rose-tinted glasses. Callie had been very strong-willed, arrogant from an early age, when she'd discovered that beauty was a source of power over the male sex. Callie would have found rejection almost impossible to accept. Callie had always been the one to do the rejecting. And she had genuinely loved Damon. Had he ever loved Callie? Did it really matter now? She would destroy those letters unread. She knew enough, had no need or desire to know any more.

All of a sudden she was far more concerned by her own behaviour. In retrospect, she perfectly understood Alex's cruelty when she had gone to his office that day with Callie. It would have been effrontery indeed had Sarah *known* that Damon was another woman's husband and the father of two young children. Small wonder that Alex had reacted incredulously to the idea that his very much married brother had given her sister an engagement ring! Nevertheless, that was what had happened.

It was that day that Sarah had learnt to hate Alex, falsely seeing him as the barrier that stood between her sister and the man she loved. But, without even suspecting it, Alex and Sarah had been talking at cross-purposes and now she knew why Alex had repeatedly condemned her own moral principles. Naturally he had believed she was encouraging Callie in her pursuit of his brother.

Losing the very foundations of hatred was a chastening experience, Sarah discovered. All that had happened since Callie's death could now be seen in a different light. Alex had wanted to protect his sister-in-law from the humiliation of that affair being exposed by the media ... quite understandably. Androula had already suffered enough. And what had Sarah done? She had threatened him and his family with tabloid exposure. Sarah winced, deeply ashamed, and yet how could she have guessed the truth when Alex assumed she already *knew* the truth?

No wonder he had called her a malicious shrew, no wonder he seethed with rage around her. Yet he had attended Callie's funeral and had probably enforced Damon's presence. And right from the outset his most overriding concern had been for Nicky. Judging Sarah to be an unacceptable guardian, Alex had been equally determined that Nicky should not suffer for the sins of his parents. In an impossible situation, Alex had tried his damnedest to remove Nicky from her care. It would have been much easier for him to offer her financial assistance towards Nicky's support and simply forget their existence. But Alex had cared too much about his nephew to be satisfied with such a conclusion.

'I am a man of my word...a man of honour.' Oh, dear lord, if that was true, where did that leave this crazy marriage she had demanded? They would have to talk, straighten out all these stupid misunderstandings, and then she would offer him an annulment. What else could she decently do?

That decision reached, Sarah felt more at peace with herself. She was reaching out to put out the light when the door opened. Her suddenly weak hand dropped back on the pillow with a dulled thud, her soft mouth opening on a soundless exclamation of disbelief.

Did Alex pause for effect in the doorway or was that her imagination? Paralysed, Sarah surveyed him from beneath her lashes. He was fully clothed... Her racing heartbeat steadied a little. He wanted to talk to her, had probably noticed her light was still on... that was all. Really, Sarah, a little voice piped up very drily, what else did you think he might be doing in your bedroom?

Alex braced two lean hands on the footboard of the bed and studied her, exactly as he had studied her that day in the hall at Gina's. Her heartbeat thumped against her breastbone in protest. I am lord of all I survey. That belief was etched unashamedly in those smouldering dark golden eyes wandering over her with a hot, earthy sensuality that was so blatant, it took her breath away.

In the fathoms-deep silence, she watched long fingers slowly travel up to his bow-tie and jerk it free, and he did not remove his intense appraisal from her expressively incredulous face for a split-second.

'No,' Sarah said breathlessly.

He cast aside the tie, shrugged wide shoulders fluidly out of his dinner-jacket and continued to watch her. A slashing smile of primal purpose curved his hard-edged mouth, the innate savagery that lay at the very heart of Alex's volatile temperament freely visible, confidently displayed. He was, she noted dazedly, very much in his element in a woman's bedroom. He unbuttoned his shirt, exposing a broad, muscular chest, golden-brown in colour and liberally sprinkled with curling black hair.

Sarah's fingers clenched tightly into the bedspread below her hand. She would stare him down if it killed her, because he just could not be serious. She rested her head to one side, striving for an appearance of cool amusement, but she could feel a blush slowly colouring up her pale skin, starting at her dry throat and moving up in an unstoppable tide.

'If you have a desire to expose yourself in a centrefold, you don't need to audition for my benefit,' Sarah commented, struggling for a tone of irony.

'You'd buy the magazine and hide it under the bed,' Alex asserted with grim amusement. 'I warned you many weeks ago that I could handle you with one hand tied behind my back...but that you wouldn't like my methods. Why didn't you listen?' Alex breathed in a velvety purr, strolling gracefully across the room to drop his shirt and his jacket across a chair.

'Your sexual machismo leaves me cold, Alex.' Sarah despised the tremor running through her voice.

'The first time we met, I noticed what beautiful eyes you had. The second time, I remember thinking, What a truly sensational pair of legs. And the third time, you let me see that glorious hair.' His accent thickened tellingly as she stared back at him, patently stunned by this wholly unexpected confession. 'You revealed yourself to me piece by exciting piece and the chemistry between us was explosive——'

'What ch-chemistry?' she stammered jerkily.

'You didn't even recognise it for what it was. You had programmed yourself to tune out all sexual messages and ignore them. But what you did feel unnerved you,' Alex murmured lazily. 'And I thought, I *want* this woman but she is the one woman I cannot have.'

'Alex ... this is a male fantasy running riot.' Her hurt and mortification that he should pretend to find her attractive were intense. 'You are trying to justify your quite unjustifiable presence in my bedroom. And shall I tell you why?'

'If you like.'

Very pale, Sarah breathed, 'I hurt your ego——'

'A bomb wouldn't deflate my ego,' Alex inserted smoothly.

'I hurt your ego,' Sarah repeated tightly, 'and you want to level the score.'

'I left scoring behind in my teens, along with not phoning when I said I would and lusting hotly after everything in a skirt between sixteen and thirty.'

'I imagine you were fairly successful,' she muttered helplessly.

'Very...but I did grow out of it and you are my wife...'

Unwarily, Sarah glanced up, registered that he wasn't wearing a stitch and hurriedly looked away, knowing that that image of Alex naked was imprinted indelibly on her memory for life. But then it had not previously occurred to her that the male physique could be that magnificent ... or that disturbing.

'I'm prepared to offer you an annulment,' she proffered in a rush, like a woman trying to bargain with an executioner at the last ditch.

'This is very sudden, isn't it?' Alex mocked. 'No.'

'I'm offering you your freedom back——'

'Are you offering me Nicky as well?'

An icy hand clutched at her heartstrings. '*No!*'

'Stalemate,' Alex said succinctly.

But, had she agreed to go and leave Nicky behind, he would have agreed to an annulment. Dear God, that was what he really wanted. This was what he had planned from the beginning and, blind idiot that she was, she had walked right into it! It had not occurred to her that Alex's offensive might be demanding his marital rights. But Alex had somehow guessed what would disturb and distress her most and Alex was prepared to play that card and utterly humiliate her in the hope that sooner or later she would take flight, leaving Nicky in his sole custody.

'I didn't *know* Damon was married!' she told him afresh.

'Your performance to that effect was certainly convincing,' Alex conceded flatly. 'But it doesn't change the fact that we're married.'

'We don't have to stay married,' she protested tautly.

Alex strode into the bathroom without responding. He wasn't listening to her.

Sarah flopped back against the pillows like a rag doll and crammed a hand against her convulsing mouth and bit back a sob of very real fear. The mere prospect of Alex enforcing sexual intimacy as a weapon appalled her. The thought of him looking at her naked, seeing all her deficiencies, touching her with cold, humiliating hands while doubtless having to fantasise about some other woman just to keep him aroused ... it terrified and tortured her.

She listened to the water beating down on the tiles in the shower and cringed. She knew she didn't have beautiful eyes or sensational legs and she also knew what he didn't know but would soon find out. What you saw wasn't what you got. Her sole claim to vanity was a padded bra, just so that she wasn't *too* noticeably flat, certainly not to draw further attention to that particular part of her body.

She felt the mattress give with his weight and curled up into a tighter, even more inaccessible ball.

A finger ran down her exposed backbone and she shuddered. 'When I said that a bomb wouldn't deflate my ego, I'm beginning to think I was deluding myself,' Alex remarked without expression.

'Please...please don't touch me. I can't give up Nicky but I'll do absolutely anything else. I'll stay out of your way...you'll never see me...you can have all the women you want!' she told him wildly.

'I want you,' Alex breathed with sudden rawness, hauling her bodily back into the hard heat of his long, powerful length with an easy strength that sent her nervous tension into overdrive.

'You cheat! You agreed to a marriage in name only!' Sarah gasped strickenly, furious that she had abandoned her pride to beg him to leave her alone and that that selfsame plea had failed to wring an ounce of compassion from him.

Alex twisted her round and pressed her flat, forcing her into glancing and unwelcome contact with gleaming golden eyes that challenged. '*When* did I agree?'

Trembling, she stared wordlessly up at him, the reality of that omission on his part only now registering with her.

'I would never have agreed to that particular term,' Alex spelt out very quietly. 'Indeed, were it not for your physical appeal, I would not have agreed to the marriage at all. Had I found you unattractive, had I not been able to imagine taking you to my bed, it would have been insanity to agree. Some day I want children of my own... Did you really believe that I would allow you to deprive me of that right as well?'

Sarah hadn't thought of that. Breathing rapidly, she looked up at him, gripped by a sinking sense of inevitability. He had accused her of tunnel vision. Guilty as charged.

'If this marriage lasts it will last on my terms, not on yours,' Alex delivered, his broad brown shoulders blocking out the light as he lowered his dark head.

Galvanised back into motion, Sarah registered his intention and made a desperate attempt to snake free of him. But Alex seemingly was prepared for evasive action and one powerful hand meshed into her hair, holding her fast. Her eyes huge, her face taut and pale, she looked up at him like a trapped animal, her heartbeat hitting the Richter scale.

His thumb massaged the curve of her jawbone almost soothingly. 'Relax.'

Was he joking?

'I won't do anything you don't want me to do,' he murmured thickly.

'Then let go of me!'

'I was about to say that I wouldn't hurt you...but that might not be true.' Dark golden eyes scanned her hungrily. 'I've never made love to a virgin before but I will be as gentle as I possibly can be.'

Hot-cheeked, she thought of denying her innocence, wondered furiously how her lack of experience could be that obvious. 'You——'

Alex rested a silencing finger against her mouth, so close now she could feel his breath on her cheek, the raw power of his all-male body resting against her. 'You set me on fire that night at Gina's house and you didn't even know it. The whole time we were in that room I was visualising how it would be if I stripped that robe from you, laid you flat and possessed you as no other man ever had...'

Sarah stared up at him in horror. 'You pervert!'

'I was very aroused,' Alex admitted huskily. 'As I was in the car after the wedding... Didn't you feel that? Can't you tell when a man wants to rip your clothes off? Don't you feel the excitement in the air... the vibrations? I looked at you and thought, She's mine now and she's woman enough—no matter what she says—to go out and make herself even more beautiful just to please me.'

Sarah was transfixed by what he was telling her, had never imagined once in her entire adult life that any man would talk to her this way. Followed by that outrageously conceited assurance that she had transformed her appearance purely to make herself more appealing for *his* benefit when no such madness had ever entered her mind, she was literally forced into speech. 'Pleasing you had nothing to do with it!'

A vibrantly amused smile slashed his sun-bronzed features. 'If you say so,' he said, with the air of an adult humouring a child over a triviality.

The astonishing charisma of that smile briefly blanked out her every rational thought. And it was while she was struggling to comprehend how a smile could make her feel all warm and dizzy that Alex kissed her, his mouth drifting down into a natural collision with hers, gentle, seeking, shorn of any threat.

But she was merely coming to terms with that astonishing gentleness when the entire tenor of his approach changed. He gave a ragged groan of impatience, she felt his hand tighten in her hair, and then his tongue delved between her softly parted lips and she shivered, lanced by a sudden startling sensation deep in the pit of her stomach. It was a clenched tight stab of shocking excitement. The pressure of his mouth increased and then circled, teased, his tongue searching out the moist interior she had instinctively opened to him.

This wasn't happening, a shattered voice screamed inside her confused mind. Alex cannot make me enjoy this, want this... need this. But she discovered that Alex could. She discovered that he could kiss her into breathless, panting surrender and leave her wanting things she had never dreamt she could want.

'You like that... I knew you would,' Alex whispered against her reddened lips, when she trembled helplessly against him and closed her eyes, feeling her body arch up as if he had programmed her response.

And he went on making expert love to her mouth, extracting her from her flimsy nightdress without her even being aware of its removal. Her hands rose of their own volition and her fingers speared into his thick black hair, loving the texture, lingering to trace his well-shaped head and finally staying to hold her to him while she moved restively, involuntarily beneath him, wanting more contact, denied it. She was in another world, a bewitching world of sensuality, aware of her body as she had never been aware of it before, aware of her capacity for pleasure and utterly seduced by the desperate need for that same pleasure to continue.

Her breasts felt tender and swollen and, when Alex splayed a hand to her spine and pulled her closer, her taut nipples came into glancing contact with his hair-roughened chest. 'Ah...' she gasped under his mouth in shock. His hands swept up her narrow ribcage and cupped her breasts and she froze, dredged from pleasure to dismay. 'No!' she cried as he released her lips.

Alex wasn't listening. Her eyes flew wide on the taut, intent look of him as he slid lithely down the bed, his hands still shaping her flesh. His dark head bent and he closed his mouth hungrily on one pouting pink nipple. Excitement tore through her in an electrifying surge, reducing the cry of denial on her tongue to a mumbled, indistinct moan. Her entire body jerked with renewed shock, her legs trembling, an ache stirring between her thighs that made her teeth grit together in a kind of agonised pleasure.

She was stripped of every thought, every feeling. The surging hunger of her own body for sensation was terrifyingly greedy. He let his tongue flick the throbbing nub and then teased her unbearably aroused flesh with his teeth while his oh, so knowing fingers played with its neglected twin and drove her even crazier. The rush of heat to her pelvis made her hips move and she cried out, moaned, gasped, flung violently out of control by the intensity of her own excitement.

His dark head lifted. Glittering golden eyes, primal in their intensity, appraised her quivering body, lingered hotly on her bared breasts and the shameless thrust of their swollen peaks, and he groaned deep in his throat with satisfaction.

'You have beautiful breasts,' he muttered raggedly, running a possessive hand over the small pouting mounds, devouring them with his heated gaze. 'And you're incredibly sensitive there...and what that does to me—*Cristos!*'

Glazed green eyes focused on him with the greatest of difficulty and she stayed an instinctive move to cover herself from his sight, momentarily as fascinated by his response as by her own. He meant what he said. He couldn't take his eyes off her. In a split-second, all the years of inadequacy and embarrassment about what she saw as her major deficiency were forgotten, banished, never to be recalled. Every remaining barrier fell away. She blossomed with a heady mix of pleasure and gratitude, rejoicing for the very first time in her own femininity.

She clashed with dark golden eyes and drowned in them. Alex lowered his head as if she had pulled him to her. He muttered something not quite steady in Greek. Gold and green meshed and she opened her arms without even thinking about it, suddenly wild to hold him close.

Somewhere in the interim, all restraint had fallen away. Alex took her mouth with shuddering force and engulfed her in *his* hunger, *his* need, *his* demands and she went under like a novice swimmer, but she was dragged down into that sexual oblivion without fear. Her last coherent thought was that if she had died without learning what he could make her feel, she would never have lived.

He trailed a forefinger along the length of one slender, extended thigh and she shivered violently in response, the raw torment of excitement instantly reclaiming her. Every nerve-ending in her body was singing wildly and then he found her, smoothly, gently explored with knowing fingers until she was ready to scream and sob, until she couldn't stay still unless he held her down, until her entire body was one vast screeching ache for the fulfilment only he could give.

Alex stared down endlessly into her rapt face, strangely hesitant in spite of the blazing hunger in his eyes and the pagan stamp of passion tautening his damp features. He parted her thighs, raised them and stilled. 'I'll hurt you,' he muttered unsteadily.

'I don't care,' she gasped, at fever pitch.

He came down on her then, took her mouth hotly, briefly and then lifted his dark head again to watch her as he entered her by slow, painful degrees. Her eyes flew wide. She was in agony and then he thrust deep into the very heart of her and the agony turned into an ecstasy of sensation so torturously intense, she almost passed out.

He began to move then, sinking his hands beneath her hips, teaching her the primal rhythm of the most mind-blowing pleasure she had ever received. He drove into her again and again, long, sure strokes of possession that threw her wildly out of control, her heartbeat crashing, her entire body centred on the explosive excitement he had generated inside her. And then, without warning, the frantic tension peaked and she was flung violently over the edge into sobbing satisfaction. She clung wildly to him, crying, 'Alex...Alex!' without even knowing what she was saying.

There were tears in her eyes and an almost child-like sense of wonder when he shuddered above her and reached the same plateau. In all her life she could never recall feeling so close to another human being. A bewildering tenderness filled her, a gut reaction she could not suppress.

She was in awe of the raw force of human passion, had never dreamt until she learnt for herself that anything could be that overwhelming, that impossible to deny. She had believed herself to be impervious to such physical needs, sensible and sexless, indeed a woman pretty much out of step with modern society, and in one shattering hour Alex had taught her that she had this extraordinary capacity for feeling...and she knew that she had been irrevocably changed forever by the experience.

Alex released her from his weight and rolled away. Instantly her hands fell back from him. She felt suddenly painfully shy and confused, at a loss in a situation new to her. She realised that she didn't feel any more married than she had felt earlier and that sexual intimacy without communication was no easier to bear simply because her lover was her husband on paper.

'Alex...I think we have to talk,' she murmured uncertainly, but forcing herself on by reminding herself how tender and considerate he had been of her inexperience.

He turned to look at her, his hooded dark eyes utterly unreadable. 'Why?'

Whatever she had expected, it had not been that single discouraging word.

'You've changed the rules as I saw them,' she persisted, struggling against the most infuriating discomfiture as she met his eyes, instantly recalling the incredible pleasure he had given her. 'Where does our...our marriage go from here?'

'But we don't have a marriage,' Alex drawled, his sensual mouth taking on a sardonic twist as if the very idea was outrageous. 'Not in the sense you suggest. I married you because I had no other choice. You gave me no other choice.'

At the reminder, Sarah paled.

'I wanted Nicky and I paid the price.'

'You said you *wanted* me,' she whispered helplessly, and a second later could have bitten her tongue out for being so honest.

'In my bed...not as my wife.'

'You wouldn't have got me any other way!' she threw back, frantically attempting to conceal the fact that she was unbelievably hurt by that blunt assurance.

Alex cast her an insolent smile that told her he was remembering just how very easy it had been for him to turn her fear and denial into willing surrender. 'You think not?'

'I told you that I didn't know that Damon was married...that both of them lied to me!' Hugging the sheet protectively to her breasts, Sarah fought to explain how she had felt after Callie's death. 'If I had known the truth, I wouldn't have felt as bitter and I wouldn't have blamed you for ruining Callie's life... Dear God, Alex, Damon told me that you had threatened to disinherit him and throw him out of the family if he married Callie! She was pregnant. Of course I blamed you, of course I hated you after the way you talked about her that day at your office——'

'What are you trying to prove to me with these lies?' In one fluidly impatient movement, Alex threw back the sheet and sprang out of bed. 'If my brother were a murderer, I wouldn't abandon him. He's family, whatever his flaws,' he spelt out succinctly. 'As to disinheriting him . . . Damon is a very wealthy young man in his own right and I have no control over his finances.'

'Then he lied about that as well,' Sarah mumbled, her attention clinging involuntarily to the long golden sweep of his back as he began to pull on his clothes. 'All right, I admit that I shouldn't have demanded that you marry me——'

'I think you wanted to catch yourself a multi-millionaire and now you want to hang on to him,' Alex said with lethal contempt. 'There has to be some reason why the real bitch routine never got off the ground!'

'How . . . how could you touch me feeling like that?' she demanded, shocked to the core by the condemnation.

'You're my wife and you'll lie down for me whenever I want,' Alex told her with devastating simplicity. 'That is my right. But outside that bedroom door you don't have any rights that I don't give you. You forced yourself on me. You have no grounds for complaint. As for your laughable assurance that you had it within your power to offer me my freedom back . . . I haven't lost my freedom. I will do whatever the hell I like whenever I like and there is nothing that you can do to stop me!'

She sat like a small statue in the vast bed, pride demanding that she should not reveal how shattered she was. But every word still found its target like a thrown knife piercing her flesh. 'I don't want to stop you,' she managed tightly, knowing that after what he had just told her there was no way she would ever share a bed with him again.

'No? You mean you weren't planning to get possessive bit by bit?' Alex prompted with derisive disbelief. 'Start asking me where I was going, when I was coming home, where I had been and throwing tantrums? I watched my father go through that with Vivien and no woman is ever going to manipulate me like that!'

So that had been why he'd planned to marry Elise. Evidently Elise would not have attached strings, would not have demanded fidelity, would not have sunk to asking awkward questions.

Sarah was in absolute turmoil because Alex had changed the terms of their marriage as she had understood them, plunging them into an intimacy she had been unprepared to handle. And now he was absolutely denying that that development should curtail his own freedom or in any way alter his lifestyle or their relationship. What relationship? she thought sickly, appalled by her own stupidity.

Alex strolled to the foot of the bed. 'And by the way, you are wasting your time with the maternal routine and Nicky,' he asserted drily. 'I'm not impressed. Why don't you just do what I expected you to do?'

Paper-pale, she whispered, 'And what was that?'

'Shop till you drop.'

Sarah bowed her head, feeling she deserved that. Dear God, how could she have abandoned every principle and spent his money even before she married him? Even Gina, not known for her scruples concerning money, had been shocked. That horrible contract and, yes, why didn't she finally admit it? After all even Alex had seen right through her.

She had wanted so badly to look her best. She had wanted so badly not to see distaste or derision in his eyes. But she had not been aware of that pitiful subconscious motivation until now and she had not been trying to attract him... had never imagined that that could be within her power.

'I shouldn't have used your money before we were married,' she mumbled with the innate honesty that was so much a part of her character.

'That pittance? I expect you to buy maybe half one dress for that amount! And why do you think you were given those cards? I was praying you would go shopping and do something with yourself.'

Somehow that made it even more humiliating. In all her life, Sarah had never felt so agonisingly, rawly vulnerable. She couldn't look at him. Her own tightly linked hands were blurring under her vision, hot, painful tears gathering in her eyes. All of a sudden she wished she were a real bitch. Maybe she could have coped better with Alex.

Alex plucked one of the flowers from the canopy above the bed and cast it on the bedspread. 'I'll be one hell of a lot easier to live with when you stop pretending to be something you're not...'

The instant the door shut on him, the dam burst. She thrust her face violently into a pillow, terrified that he might hear the shuddering sobs tearing for an exit from her shivering body. She was just so angry with herself! She was just so appalled by the extent of her own weakness!

Almost twenty-five years old and she had behaved like a sex-starved adolescent when he'd touched her. All he had had to do was tell her that he wanted her and she had been so damned grateful and flattered, she had let him make love to her! A sixteen-year-old girl, very lacking in confidence, still existed inside her—a sixteen-year-old girl who had once been very badly hurt. And that teenager still inside her had ensured that tonight she was even more badly hurt. She had told herself that she was happy to live alone, that she didn't need any man to make her life more meaningful, and she had begun to believe that, denying her own loneliness, denying that she had sexual feelings and needs like other women. She had felt safe that way. She hadn't had to open herself up to the risk of being hurt again. She had convinced herself that she was single by choice, not single because no man who ever attracted her asked her out...but that was closer to reality.

Alex was gorgeous but she had blocked that awareness with the ease of long practice. It had not occurred to her that he could find her attractive and instinctively she had refused to admit or recognise that his devastating good looks and powerful physical presence were affecting her. But Alex had read her like an open book. Alex had known that she was his for the asking before he'd even laid a finger on her. Alex was highly sexed and very experienced, easily able to pick up on and interpret a woman's response to him . . . even if that same woman was too naïve to know that she was putting out that response.

Now she had to live with the knowledge that Alex had invaded her bed purely because he saw that as his right. For some peculiar reason, best known to himself, Alex did find her physically attractive. But that was her only appeal and not something she could even feel marginally good about in the light of his subsequent behaviour. Alex was still seething over the fact that she had demanded that he marry her and only a very stupid woman would have let her guard drop to the extent she had.

Alex thought she had used an innocent baby to trap herself a very rich husband. He didn't believe that she loved Nicky. He didn't believe that his brother had told such outrageous lies . . . in fact, he didn't much want to hear anything about what had motivated her before their marriage. He didn't seem to believe a single thing she said. Indeed, he fondly imagined she was putting on some silly act to try and impress him and bring him round to the idea that their marriage might have a real future.

She couldn't win against odds like that. She would be damned if she was a bitch and damned if she wasn't. In anguish, she thought back painfully to her hideously mortifying response to his lovemaking. Even though her experience with men was severely limited, she had forgotten the one fact she did know. Men always wanted sex. Men were just programmed that way. And just because Alex was gorgeous and rich and spoilt for choice when it came to satisfying his sexual needs it didn't mean Alex was one whit different from any of the other men who had tried to pounce on her.

No, she thought sickly, the only thing different about Alex was that he had succeeded where the others had failed. Succeeded effortlessly, too. Her swollen face burned hot. And then he got out of bed, the conquering hero, the gentleman that he wasn't, and he tore her apart and he made her feel cheap and stupid and outstandingly naïve because she had actually believed that he had changed towards her in some way.

Nothing had ever hurt so much. Her pride, she told herself. He had ground it to dust. Well, he would never do it again, she swore to herself. She had married him to be a mother to Nicky and nothing he could do was going to prevent her from carrying out that role. She sniffed, scrabbled for another tissue. Alex was a cruel, heartless bastard and she would never ever forget what he had done to her tonight!

CHAPTER SEVEN

'Who is the most handsome boy in the world? Who has the most *gorgeous* brown eyes and silky black hair?' Sarah whispered, lying on her stomach on the carpet, as smilingly intent on Nicky, who was kicking and waving his arms, as Nicky was intent on her. 'And you're not going to grow up and kiss the girls to make them cry, are you?' she sighed. 'I want you to be sensitive and loving and romantic. It takes a *real* man to be those things...don't you ever listen to anybody telling you different——'

'Is this a private indoctrination session or can anyone join in?'

Sarah froze, her head jerking up to focus in horror on Alex's hand-stitched Italian leather shoes. Dear heaven, how could it be that time already? She always made sure she was well out of the way during Alex's visits to the nursery. And as a rule she was very efficient in her timing. In the past two weeks, she had actually gone forty-eight hours twice without even laying eyes on Alex in the distance. With a little effort, it wasn't difficult. Alex was a creature of habit and routine as regards his working day, and the hours he set aside for becoming acquainted with his nephew were equally regular.

Feeling dreadfully ill at ease, her face hotly flushed, Sarah lifted up on to all fours and then back on to her heels. Then she discovered that squinting up at Alex from that angle merely made him more intimidating and she hurriedly sprang upright, skimming taut hands down over her jean-clad hips, tugging at the T-shirt, still damp

114

from Nicky's bath, conscious that it was clinging to her braless breasts.

'If you turn him into a sensitive, loving, romantic guy,' Alex drawled with lashings of sarcasm, 'he'll be a pushover for every gold-digger in Europe.'

'I don't see why,' she muttered helplessly, staring at his scarlet silk tie. 'Those kind of p-personality traits do not exclude intelligence and caution——'

'They do in my book.' Alex released his breath in a sudden hiss. 'Look at me...'

Sarah swallowed hard and did so. And that ghastly weak-at-the-knees sensation took over just as she had feared it would. She connected with dark golden eyes and the world started to spin and her mind went terrifyingly blank. Worse, every quivering skin cell went shamelessly on red alert. She had worked incredibly hard at willing these things to stop happening to her, but so far she could not feel that success was within reach. It was gruesome...all her life to have rejoiced in supreme self-control and then to be presented with Armageddon in the shape of a mere male.

Every time she looked at Alex he got more gorgeous. She searched for a flaw and couldn't find one. She reminded herself of how in every field he failed her standards for the mythical ideal man and still she was plunged into this appallingly adolescent state of sexual awareness every time he came within ten feet of her! She felt like an arsonist holding dry paper, desperate for the match to ignite her conflagration.

No...nobody had ever told her and she had never dreamt that her thoughts and her reactions could rove so violently out of her control. But somehow Alex had done this to her in *one* night... Dear heaven, if he was to approach her again, what devastation might he then leave in his wake? She reminded herself that Alex had had his revenge. He had made love to her. He had asserted his truly unforgivable conviction that she had no rights whatsoever over her own body. Why on earth should he want to do it again?

It occurred to her that Alex's gaze had turned pure gold and in addition to his extraordinarily long silence his eyes were wandering over her slowly but with sizzling intensity. Alarm bells went off madly inside her head. Sarah dredged her eyes from his and dropped them, but that was a mistake . . . She noticed, absolutely could not help but notice that Alex was unmistakably in a state of sexual arousal.

Her face so hot it could have doubled for a frying-pan on fire, Sarah tore shocked but dismayingly fascinated eyes from the alarmingly tight fit of Alex's superbly tailored trousers and, at speed, bent down, scooped up Nicky and hurriedly planted him back into his cot.

'I decided to finish early . . .'

'Oh,' Sarah muttered.

'We could have dinner together,' Alex murmured lazily.

And guess what the after-dinner entertainment is? she thought with a staggering mix of reactions to the under-written threat. A wave of blinding heat zapped through her, leaving her dizzy. Only then did the shame and self-loathing make itself felt. Just the very thought of Alex touching her again sent her emotions haywire but every haywire reaction could be traced right back to a burst of anticipation that was utterly wanton and without conscience.

'I've already eaten.' Since Alex hadn't eaten dinner once in his own home in two weeks, Sarah had taken to having a tray in her room, finding the solitary splendour of the dining-room far too much to handle with at least two staff fighting to serve her and showing in a variety of little ways that, for some peculiar reason best known to themselves, they sympathised with so neglected a new bride.

In fact, staff relations, something which Sarah had worried about, were astonishingly good. She, who had never dealt with a servant in her life, was treated like royalty. Her favourite meals, her favourite flowers...anything she expressed the smallest desire or liking for magically appeared with beaming smiles. She was still wondering just why the cast of thousands Alex employed to maintain the château should be so incredibly nice to her.

'You could keep me company,' Alex drawled in the sizzling silence.

Those vibrations he had once mentioned were invisibly lancing through the atmosphere like lightning bolts. Sarah trembled, unnerved, wanting to run...wanting to stay, torn apart.

'And if I was to say please...?' Alex prompted thickly.

The no-good swine, she reflected abruptly, humiliation devouring her alive. For two weeks you're the invisible woman. Then he feels like sex late one afternoon and all of a sudden you're flavour of the day! Dear God, it was just so *disgusting* to be sexually turned on by a male like Alex Terzakis. It made her want to have a bath and scrub herself raw.

As every scrap of colour faded from her face, she raised an unsteady hand to her literally pounding temples and said, 'I don't feel well,' with perfect truth. This amount of tension was bad for her. It gave her a headache.

Studying the carpet, she uttered a stifled screech as she was abruptly lifted off her feet. 'What are you doing?' she gasped.

'You should lie down——'

'No! When I've got a headache, I walk around...g-go outside, get some fresh air!' Sarah stammered in a frantic tone.

A foot over the doorway of the nursery, Alex paused and looked down at her. It was lethal. One second she was rigid, the next she was melted honey on its way to boiling-point. The heat of him, his heartbeat, the feel of his arms around her and the unforgettable scent of his skin... 'Please put me down,' she mumbled, fighting a rearguard action to the effect of those astonishingly bright eyes of his.

'You should have engaged another nanny as I instructed. You've been overworking.'

Nanny Brown had lasted precisely three days after the wedding, taking her leave in high dudgeon the morning she dared to tell Alex that he was interfering with her routine by showing up before breakfast-time in the nursery. Sarah hadn't been present but Claudine, the young, pleasant girl hired to assist in Nicky's care, had been and evidently Alex had blown a fuse and Nanny, mightily offended, had informed him that he didn't need to sack her, she was leaving to take up employment with some titled couple, who had seemingly offered her the sun, the moon and the stars to come to them instead.

'Nonsense...' Lost in the depths of his eyes, Sarah stopped breathing.

Alex loosed a kind of strangled groan and took her mouth so hotly that she scorched in shock, unprepared for a frontal assault of such blatancy. His tongue drove between her lips, searching out the moist interior, and an electrifying excitement shot through her, leaving her weak with longing.

The world spun faster and faster. Coloured lights shot through the blackness behind her lowered eyelids. Her hand lifted and her fingers dug into his luxuriant black hair. At last she was *alive* again after two weeks hovering on the brink of inglorious extinction.

Abruptly, Alex tore his mouth from hers. A dark tide of blood accentuated his hard cheekbones. He looked shattered, frustrated, outraged. 'What the hell are you doing to me?' he growled without warning, dumping her down on the ground again so fast that she had to sag against the wall to stay upright.

'Me?' It was the most she could manage, planting shaking hands to the wall to steady herself, her temperature still rocketing tempestuously at fever point.

Alex was breathing rapidly. His gaze dropped below the level of her chin to the visible thrust of her nipples beneath the T-shirt. He swore fluently, violently, the brown hand that she could see suddenly sweeping up between them. He grabbed a handful of T-shirt to haul her closer, frightening her out of her wits.

'You wear a bra outside the bedroom,' he grated down at her. 'And you swim in two pieces of bikini. And you sunbathe in the same two pieces. Is that clear?'

Soundlessly she nodded. You didn't argue with a madman. It just didn't seem the time to tell him that she couldn't swim and hadn't yet taken the time to sunbathe.

'You don't flaunt yourself like this!' Alex derided. 'Now go to bed. You have a headache, go to bed...'

Sarah backed away slow step by slow step, lest a sudden move might push him further over the edge of such illogical and utterly incomprehensible behaviour. Flaunt herself? What on earth was he talking about? Her cheeks burned. She wore the least possible clothing for Nicky's bathtime. Not yet as polished as Claudine at bathing her nephew, Sarah invariably got pretty wet and it got so hot in the nursery bathroom with the heating going full blast lest Nicky contract a chill.

At the top of stairs, she glanced back. Alex had returned to the nursery. She wished she could spy on him the way he had spied on her. Did Alex talk baby-talk? Or was it more along the MCP line of 'think of all the women out there, all the conquests, all the entertainment available'? Sarah pulled a face. It was to be hoped that Alex had more wit in his conversation with Nicky then he had with the toys that kept on appearing by the day. Did he really think Nicky would soon be playing with that incredible train set in the playroom next door to the nursery? And what about the bike? And the talking teddy with the maniacal laugh that made Nicky scream blue murder?

Sarah sagged down on her own bed, knowing she was being unjust. But the truth was she had not been prepared for Alex to take such an interest in Nicky. Instead she got this image of Alex haunting toyshops ... Alex, patently ignorant of the stages of child development, purchasing anything and everything which took his fancy and bringing it home to Nicky. On some level she didn't want to examine, something twisted inside her when she pictured Alex in a toyshop, too arrogant to ask advice but trying so hard all the same.

More and more, she was having to acknowledge that on yet another point she had misjudged Alex. He did fully intend to be a father to Nicky. He did genuinely seem to love his nephew. In short, Alex was in possession of a whole set of more appealing characteristics than he would ever trouble to show to his unwanted wife.

Sarah groaned, realising that she had left the book she was reading downstairs. Alex would still be with Nicky.

But Alex, she soon discovered, wasn't with Nicky. She was descending the main staircase when she heard Vivien's voice, shrill and furious, leaking through the ajar door of the library.

'...none of my business when you have a wife and a child to consider? If you think that I am about to stand by while you humiliate that girl, Alex——'

'You talk of something of which you know nothing,' Alex responded with icicles freezing from every syllable.

'Your father was always discreet ... he never embarrassed me in public——'

'Something more than can have been said for you where he was concerned,' Alex whipped back.

'I'm sorry...' Vivien's voice sounded choked. 'I'm sorry that you can remember that.'

Frozen on the staircase, Sarah strained her ears but couldn't catch what Alex said next. It was too quiet. What the heck was Vivien doing interfering? No doubt in a well-meaning spirit, wanting all to be hunky-dory in her stepson's marriage, but didn't she realise how bitterly Alex would resent it?

Sarah went back upstairs without her book. What was Alex doing to humiliate her? Did she really want to know? Why should she care? It was none of her business what he got up to outside the château... But as sternly as she told herself that came the stark disagreement of her own feelings.

Alex had changed the rules of their marriage. Alex had made their relationship personal and intimate and whether she liked it or not Sarah could no longer think of him enjoying his much vaunted freedom without feeling her stomach cramp with nausea. Gone were the heady days when she'd gaily written off the idea of Alex's sleeping around as being nothing to do with her. In fact, right now, it felt like a very big central issue in her life and common sense and practicality put no curb on that unwelcome reality.

Night after night, Alex came home and went straight back out again and Sarah didn't know where he went or what he did when he got there. Nor would she have asked, after what he had hurled at her on the wedding night. Charming as Sarah had found Vivien, Vivien had evidently in the past carried on in such a way about her late husband's infidelity that the whole family must have suffered greatly. Certainly Alex had. With derision he had enumerated all his personal hates in a women: getting possessive, keeping tabs on his every movement and throwing tantrums. Vivien must have been seriously guilty of all three sins and she had not had the sensitivity

to wage her war with her erring husband behind closed
doors.

Alex had mapped out his future with a bride he had
calculated to be as different as she could possibly be from
his stepmother. Unemotional, uninvolved. That had been
Alex's ideal marriage. The hatching of a dynasty and all
the freedom he could want on the side. A detached relationship in which only the barest necessities would have
to be shared. Sarah shuddered. Alex was capable of so
much more... wasn't he?

Her head now really was aching fit to burst. She lay
down, feeling suddenly foolishly tearful. What was
wrong with her? But she knew... didn't she? She was
involved, much more involved with Alex than she had
ever planned to be and it was all his fault. If he had left
her alone, the marriage would have been a total sham
and she wouldn't have minded then, would she?

Or would she have? How long could she have lived in
Alex's radius without becoming aware that she fancied
him something rotten with all the lack of control of an
adolescent suffering from a severe crush? Alex didn't
need to go out and bed-hop to humiliate her, she decided. She was being humiliated enough by the feelings
he had awakened inside her, promptings that day by day
were casting her into ever deeper turmoil.

About an hour later, a knock sounded on her door.
Alex appeared. Sarah snatched the bedding all the way
up to her throat. His sensual mouth tightened, sparks
flaring gold in his dark eyes. He set a glass down beside
her bed.

'What's that?' she demanded, as if it might be rat
poison.

If possible, Alex stiffened even more. 'Something to
take your headache away.'

Sarah surveyed him in helpless amazement. 'You
brought me something for my sore head?'

'I fail to see why the fact should fill you with such rampant disbelief!' Alex roared at her without warning, the syllables splintering with sudden temper. 'I can be as considerate and sensitive as the next man . . . !'

Attila the Hun? Vivien, it seemed, had left her mark on a temperament that was volatile to say the least. Sarah stretched out a blind hand, lifted the glass, downed the contents and choked. Brandy, enough to knock out a bull elephant. Fire hurtled down her throat and into her stomach. Tears streaming from her eyes, she breathed again.

'It's good for period pain,' Alex told her.

Sarah's jaw dropped. Her skin flamed.

'Don't be such a prude,' Alex muttered impatiently. 'I know more about PMT than nine out of ten men. Vivien saw to that.'

'I don't get PMT,' Sarah asserted shakily. 'And I actually just had a headache.'

Alex shrugged a broad shoulder, his startlingly handsome features impassive, temper back under lock and key. He studied her for several unbearably tense seconds and then strode over the windows, tugging back a curtain and opening one. 'It's too stuffy in here,' he complained.

The silence stretched.

'I think we ought to have a party.'

'A *party*?'

'It's time you were introduced to family and friends.'

Vivien had been busy. Sarah swallowed hard on her distaste at that fact. 'I didn't think you intended to——'

Alex swung back so fast, she was still speaking. 'Intended to what?'

'Introduce me to anybody,' she muttered tightly. 'And quite frankly I don't think it's a good idea. Much better just to go on as we are and people would soon get the message that I'm a bit like Mr Rochester's crazy wife in the attic, never seen, never mentioned——'

'Mr Rochester's what?' Alex demanded blankly.

'*Jane Eyre*...maybe you haven't read it.'

'I did not put you in the attic,' Alex breathed with sudden renewed ferocity.

'No, but let's not pretend that I'm the sort of wife you precisely want to show off.' Sarah thrust her chin high to prove that she was unhurt by that reality.

'I am not ashamed of you.' Dull coins of colour lay over his cheekbones.

A lump lodged in her tight throat. Damn Vivien, she thought painfully. 'Look, why can't we be honest about this? I *know* that you are cringing at the thought of having to march me out for public display, Alex——'

'Rubbish!' He dealt her a smouldering look of anger. 'That is complete and utter——!' He spat out an expletive and Sarah stiffened, offended by his language. He drove a not quite steady hand through his black hair and then threw up both hands in a gesture of raw frustration. 'I'm sorry,' he finally vented. 'But I have not given you cause to accuse me of that.'

Sarah released a jerky laugh. 'We got married at the most unearthly hour of the day in the darkest, most unfashionable corner of London you could find. You walked through the airport three paces in front of me——'

'Two weeks ago, I was still very angry. I wanted to be sure you would not enjoy our wedding-day.'

'I didn't.' Sarah studied her tightly linked hands, sensing that she was at some kind of crossroads with Alex and not knowing how honest to be. 'Look...I know the right knives and forks to use because I used to be a silver waitress in a hotel. I also used to scrub floors. In fact every job I've ever had was in some menial capacity. I'm really quite happy to stay in the attic, metaphorically speaking, as long as I have Nicky. I don't want you gritting your teeth and trying not to wince every time I embarrass you...I would really hate that.'

'You don't embarrass me,' Alex framed very quietly. 'A woman as beautiful as you could never embarrass me.'

Sarah released a groan. 'Alex, ditch the soft soap,' she urged. 'You and I both know that we come from different worlds and that if it weren't for that baby upstairs we'd never have met——'

'But we did meet and we did marry,' Alex cut in with ruthless bite.

Sarah wrinkled her small nose. 'You can have a divorce any time you want on any terms——'

'And you'd bloody well like that, wouldn't you?' Alex ripped back at her with sudden raw hostility, smouldering anger igniting the atmosphere again.

Her head was starting to thump again and, dear lord, but she was tired. Flopping down, she turned over, drained of arguments. Talking to Alex wasn't like talking to other people. It was like a mental assault course, spiced by ever bigger and more daunting obstacles and his incomprehensible bursts of temper.

'A separation?' she tried weakly. 'I could live somewhere close and you could see as much of Nicky as you liked——?'

'No.' It was thunderous, final, full of suppressed outrage that she could dare to suggest such a solution.

'I don't see why not,' she admitted out loud. 'We might as well be separated anyway, living in this great house.'

'I intend to rectify that situation.' Glittering golden eyes pounced on her, lingered, threatened in a blaze of stormy appraisal. 'Perhaps when you have a child of your own you'll feel a little less flighty.'

'*A child of my own*?' All of a sudden, Sarah felt considerably less sleepy, studying him with wide, disbelieving eyes.

'Why not?' Alex challenged with dark, lethal cool but a distinct aura of threat about his aggressive stance.

'I can think of a hundred reasons why not!' Sarah told him.

'I can't think of one. You're so obsessed with Nicky, it's unhealthy.'

'Unhealthy?'

'For you, the world outside that nursery does not exist,' Alex drawled harshly.

'But why should that bother you?' she asked in genuine confusion.

Alex looked heavenwards like a male in torment. Then he breathed out and strode forward with a disturbing air of purpose. He flipped the bedding back off her.

'*Alex*!' she gasped.

A pair of powerful arms snatched her up off the mattress. 'You can nurse your headache in my bed tonight...and every other night,' he asserted fiercely.

'Put me down!' she shouted at him furiously. 'Have you gone mad?'

Letting rip with something that she had no doubt was exceedingly rude in his own language, Alex wrenched open the door and carried her, kicking and fighting, down the corridor. Sarah went crazy. 'You're a maniac!' she screeched at him at the top of her voice. 'I offer you the divorce or the separation that you should be gasping for and you go ballistic!'

Crushing her to his broad chest to still her frantic struggles, Alex slung her a filthy look. 'You noticed?' he queried darkly, between clenched even white teeth. 'Well, then, you're learning. I am wildly encouraged by such astute observative powers.'

He kicked open a door, strode across a well-lit room and deposited her on a bed. Sarah was up like a deer and off that mattress before he had even straightened but Alex blocked her passage back to the door.

'Get out of my way,' Sarah told him unsteadily, hitching the sliding strap of her embarrassingly thin, slinky nightdress back on to one pale shoulder.

The movement was a mistake. Alex's golden gaze flamed over her small, slight figure, every slender curve of which was blatantly revealed by the light behind her. He backed a step and turned the key in the lock.

She couldn't believe her eyes. 'How can you be so childish?'

'I have no intention of chasing you round the château for the entertainment of our staff.' Alex pocketed the key. 'Why don't you get into bed?'

'Because I refuse to share a bed with you!' Sarah drew herself up to her full height, pride, self-preservation and innate obstinacy evident in every inch of her bearing.

'You sleep here from now on,' Alex delivered flatly, tenaciously. 'In my bed.'

Sarah squared her shoulders. Wanting him was one thing, condoning that weak shameful craving another. She had promised herself that she would never allow him to use her again and she intended to keep that promise. 'I am not the kind of woman who just does what you tell her when you snap your fingers,' she said witheringly..

His night-dark eyes slashed into her. 'Then allow me to explain your position,' Alex murmured, his voice frighteningly quiet and low in pitch. 'If you don't get into my bed, I'll rip off that nightdress and do what I am burning to do...so thoroughly and so often, you won't be fit to get back out of that bed for at least twenty-four hours.'

Sarah's tongue shot out to wet her dry lips.

'On the other hand, if you do get into bed, I'll struggle manfully to respect your headache...'

Sarah shot into bed without another word. Meek as a lamb, she conceded furiously, but then heroism in the face of overwhelming odds would not have brought its own reward. It would have been another dose of humiliation, she reminded herself. Sex that was just sex was not a practice she had any desire to take up on a regular basis.

Alex reached for her several minutes later.

'Don't!' she launched over her shoulder.

'If you don't shut up,' Alex whispered silkily, forcing her close with hard, strong hands, 'I'll forget I ever made such a self-sacrificing concession as letting you lie here untouched...'

She stopped breathing. The heat of his body, the incredibly intimate feel of him against her trembling body warned her that Alex was not joking... he was very aroused. Reaching out, he turned off the light. Hot as hellfire, she lay there in the darkness.

'And if you can't stop moving about in that wonderfully encouraging way, you had better start praying...'

Hardly breathing and not moving, she lay there, fighting the flood of heat warming her and the wanton stab of excitement tugging low in the pit of her stomach. She just didn't understand Alex Terzakis; she just didn't understand him at all. And, for a female who liked to know exactly where she stood at all times, that was a terrifying admission.

CHAPTER EIGHT

'Up!'

The next morning, some horribly cruel character trailed the bedding off Sarah, letting in a cold draught.

She opened her eyes to see Alex, fully dressed and breathtakingly immaculate in a beautifully tailored navy suit. 'Up?' she whispered weakly. 'What time is it?'

'Seven. And, like a good little wife, you are going to get up and have breakfast with me...' With absolute sadism, Alex lifted her and dumped her in a heap on the stool in front of the dressing-table. 'You brush your hair, wash your face and come downstairs.'

Shivering with cold and the rudeness of her awakening, Sarah grimaced. She liked to wake up slowly and peacefully, rising in her own time.

'You're like a zombie at this hour, aren't you?' Alex thrust a brush in her hand.

'I have no dressing-gown.'

'Have mine.' Determined not to be circumvented, Alex took it upon himself to thread her arms into the sleeves and fold it round her. Helpfully, he tied the sash and rolled up the cuffs.

'I look ridiculous.'

'Who cares?'

Thrust into the bathroom, she groaned. She had barely slept the previous night and now the torture had started with the dawn chorus. What was the matter with Alex? Did a vein of insanity run in the Terzakis genes? Hadn't she given him what he said he wanted? Hadn't she left him alone, stayed out of his path? Most unfaithful husbands would kill for that sort of freedom. So why was

129

Alex suddenly and inexplicably demanding that she do *wifely* things like sharing the same bed and breakfast-table?

'I won't be home tonight...' Alex informed her.

Sarah didn't bat an eyelash. She wondered why he was bothering to tell her.

'I will be in Geneva until tomorrow.'

A long, simmering silence stretched.

'Do you have any interest in my movements?' Alex enquired very, very quietly.

None. She wouldn't allow herself to have an interest. She wanted to think of Alex as Nicky's uncle, not as her husband. In fact, she flatly refused to think of him as her husband. Her clear emerald eyes gleamed. 'Do you want me to take an interest?'

His strong jawline hardened. Golden eyes flashed. Thrusting back his chair, he tossed aside his napkin. 'I'll see you tomorrow.'

Sarah cleared her throat and asked a question that had been nibbling anxiously at the back of her mind for several days. 'Alex...?'

He studied her with unhidden impatience.

'When is Damon planning to come and see Nicky?' she completed tautly.

Alex stilled, clearly taken by surprise. 'He has had an open invitation since the day of our wedding.'

Sarah took a deep breath. 'Is it me? Is that why he hasn't come?'

'I really have no idea. Naturally it will not be an easy meeting for either of you,' Alex acknowledged. 'Although a little more honesty on your part might simplify matters.'

'On my part?'

'I'm prepared to concede that *you* were not aware that Damon was a married man. But I will not accept that he ever asked your sister to marry him——'

'He did,' Sarah said tightly.

'Or,' Alex continued, 'that he left your sister without means of support.'

'He did,' she said again.

'I won't believe that,' Alex asserted grimly. 'Money would have been the easiest thing of all for him to give to salve his conscience. He knew that the cheque I gave was never cashed. When you decide to face the truth of that affair, maybe then I will think the time is right to encourage Damon more actively to visit us here.'

'I am not lying.' Furiously conscious that he did not believe her, Sarah stared back at him, taut with frustration. Without proof, she knew she had no hope of convincing Alex of her innocence. First and foremost he would choose to believe his brother, but it angered Sarah that Alex should continue to harbour this view of her as an outright liar. Angered and hurt, she registered. Did that mean Alex's opinion mattered to her? She was shaken by the awareness that it did.

Alex sent her a glittering golden glance. 'For Nicky's sake, I am prepared to make certain sacrifices.'

'Sacrifices?' she questioned without understanding.

His dark, strong face hardened. 'I have seen for myself that, whatever other flaws you may have, you love that child and will undoubtedly be a more loving mother to him than any other woman I might have married.'

The compliment with the scorpion's sting in its tail. Her teeth gritted together, angry pink washing her cheeks. How dared he talk about *his* sacrifices and *her* flaws?

'And for that reason I have decided to do everything within my power to make this marriage work,' Alex concluded arrogantly.

'You actually ate dinner at home last night,' Sarah agreed sarcastically.

His savage cheekbones clenched, an arc of colour highlighting his shimmering eyes. 'I expect you to make the same effort,' he delivered, ignoring the ungenerous stab.

'Not on your terms,' Sarah returned, her injured pride simmering towards boiling-point.

'On my terms or not at all.'

Sarah stared blindly back at him, knowing she could not survive those terms. He was finally telling her why she was now expected to share his bed on a permanent basis. Dear God, how could any mere woman live with such an honour? Alex Terzakis had made an unbelievably magnificent gesture, a sacrifice of immense magnitude: he was willing to accept Sarah as his wife. I really have arrived, she told herself sarcastically, but there was this terrible pain in among the anger and the wounded pride and she couldn't understand the pain.

'I can't accept your terms,' she whispered finally.

His terms would break her. Instinct told her that. To share his bed and rejoice in his passion without love or respect or even fidelity would demean her. Nor would having his children ease that humiliation. Her bitterness and resentment would inevitably triumph and there would be no happiness for either of them in such an arrangement.

'If you don't, I'll divorce you...'

Shattered, Sarah looked back at him. Alex stared back, not a muscle moving on his darkly handsome face, his impassive dark eyes reading her sudden pallor.

'And I will ensure that Nicky stays with me.'

Appalled, Sarah rose shakily upright. 'You can't do that!'

'As you once said to me, money talks,' Alex drawled with dark satire. 'And, in the light of the pre-nuptial contract you signed, I'm sure you recall that if the marriage breaks down for whatever reason you'll be lucky to get your train fare home!'

Her legs wouldn't hold her up any longer. Slowly she sank down again, simply gaping at him in horror. She had never dreamt that Alex could be this cruel, was quite unprepared for such ruthless tactics being employed against her. He attacked on her weakest flank without remorse. He knew how much she loved Nicky. He was using a sledge-hammer on a nut. Surely her presence in his bed could not be this important to him? She remembered that he had said that he wanted children. Was that why? In a frantic surge of feverish mental activity, she saw a way out.

'If you want children we could use IVF.'

Alex looked back at her blankly.

Hesitantly, the words tumbling out of her, she rushed to explain the marvels of technology and the complete lack of necessity for any actual physical contact.

Alex stood there, frozen to the spot, apparently thrown violently by the suggestion that he could father his future family without ever laying a hand on his wife.

Abruptly, a lean brown hand lifted to silence her. Narrowed dark eyes welded to hers, Alex breathed, 'Are you trying to tell me that I must approach a laboratory to get you pregnant?'

Sarah reddened but pressed on, her sole ambition to show him that they need not participate in sexual intimacy simply to produce a child. She marvelled that Alex appeared so ignorant of such processes. 'That way we could abide by the original terms of our marriage,' she pointed out breathlessly.

All of a sudden she registered that it was not ignorance that had silenced Alex but a kind of unholy and incredulous fascination backed by rather daunting signs of gathering rage. A dark tide of blood had flushed his golden features, a tiny muscle tugging relentlessly at the corner of his eloquent mouth. 'You have to be out of your mind to suggest such a thing to me!' he told her rawly.

'Alex . . . if we could for once move away from this macho conditioning of yours and talk about this sensibly, you might see that it is actually a very sane solution to the problem.'

Alex strode forward and pulled her up out of her seat with two powerful hands. 'My children are not going to be conceived in a test tube and that has nothing to do with my "macho conditioning",' he spelt out ferociously. 'When you first opened the subject, I thought you were joking, I could not credit that you could be serious.'

Sarah made no pointless attempt to escape. One lesson she had learnt. Alex was considerably stronger than she was. She stood there, icily composed on the surface, a teeming mass of growing agitation underneath. 'I do not want to sleep with you,' she stated. 'That is a sacrifice I am not prepared to make——'

'You bitch...' After a startled moment, Alex let loose in Greek, his fluent English letting him down as he stared down at her in savage fury, as white beneath his dark tan as though she had struck him.

'I don't know why you should take that personally, Alex,' she said tremulously. 'It's not as though we have feelings for each other like other married people——'

'I have some very powerful feelings for you!' One dark hand clenched round her forearm, Alex trailed her over to the door. The pilot of his helicopter was hovering in readiness. He broke into speech about the lateness of the hour.

'I will catch a later flight,' Alex bit out.

'Let go of me,' Sarah spat on the way up the stairs. 'What the heck do you think you're doing?'

Out of sight of the hall, she attempted to jerk free of his bruising grasp. 'Stop it!' she burst out hotly.

His hand tightened and a fuse blew inside Sarah. Her other hand flew up as she stopped, intending to fetch him a wallop that would flatten him. Alex parried that furious hand and reacted by clamping his hands to her waist instead and hoisting her into a fireman's lift.

'You *swine*!' she screeched. 'Put me down this minute!'

He put her down on his bed and came down so fast on top of her that she had no time to react. 'You're my wife and I want to make love to you,' he spelt out fiercely.

'Be assured that if anything happens it will be rape!' Sarah spat up at him.

Pinning her flat, Alex undid the sash on the dressing-gown, peeled it wide.

'I'll never forgive you if you do this,' she swore strickenly. She collided with glinting golden eyes and something twisted in pleasurable pain in the pit of her stomach. Shakily she gasped in oxygen under the shattering onslaught of that all-pervasive stare. Naked panic filled her to overflowing.

'No, it's yourself you won't forgive,' Alex murmured softly, intently, scanning the myriad expressions skimming her triangular face. 'All that stands between us is your pride and your need to be in control. And in my bed you are out of control.'

Appalled by his insight, Sarah shot a look of loathing up at him. 'I hate you, Alex.'

He tugged the dressing-gown down her arms. 'I don't think so,' he said in a velvety purr. 'I think you want me so much it terrifies you.'

'Naturally you would like to think that——'

'*Know* it, not think it,' Alex countered, shrugging out of his jacket and pitching it carelessly aside, yanking at his tie with a not quite steady hand. 'You excite the hell out of me. You really can't expect me not to know that it's mutual——'

'It is not mutual!' Her teeth ground together.

'Our wedding night was unforgettably erotic,' Alex savoured, peeling off his shirt. 'I've thought of little else for two endless weeks. In fact I only have to think about what being inside you felt like and I——'

Crimson-cheeked, Sarah snapped, 'Shut up!'

Alex smiled with lethal amusement, all temper banished by lust, she assumed, and his superior position. 'And the wonder of finding a woman of your age so innocent and shy had a charm and an appeal I never thought to experience. Why were you still a virgin?'

'I stayed away from macho pigs like you!'

'Maybe on some level you knew I was in your future,' Alex drawled with unashamed conceit.

'If I'd known,' Sarah practically shrieked at him, 'I'd have come into your office with a shotgun!'

'And I find that even more attractive,' Alex delivered with mocking amusement. 'All of my adult life, your sex have gone to extraordinary lengths to please me. I've been chased, flattered and encouraged by every woman I ever wanted since I was fifteen.'

'You conceited toad!' Sarah launched at him.

'Then you came along and for the very first time I was challenged and, believe me, I was very challenged keeping my hands off you until our wedding night. I didn't want you to bolt. That's why I didn't come near you during the weeks before our marriage.'

Sarah was in such a rage, she was almost incoherent. 'You conniving, cunning, sneaky——!'

Alex laughed softly, spontaneously, and pressed a warning forefinger to the fullness of her lower lip, silencing her. 'I lay in my bed at night thinking about what it would be like to have you under me and it surpassed my every expectation. That fiery spirit which makes you so damned mouthy, that stubborn streak a mile wide which makes you persist even when you haven't a hope in hell of winning . . . when that translates into passion, you're every fantasy I've ever had in my bed!'

His satisfaction was obvious. Her small hands balled into fists. 'Alex, get off me!' she shouted.

Alex slid down the zip on his trousers with a flourish and grinned at her, suddenly startlingly younger in his raw amusement than she had ever seen him. The phone started ringing. Alex bent back and lifted the receiver without releasing her limbs from his weight.

'No more calls,' he said and dropped it back again.

'I want you to let me go,' Sarah framed, putting every atom of authority she could muster into the demand.

'So it took me a couple of weeks to settle down into the idea of being married,' Alex murmured huskily, a bare brown shoulder shifting in an infinitesimal shrug, dark golden eyes resting on her hungrily, 'a couple of weeks to come to terms with the fact that I had a wife who makes the perfect mistress . . . a little mental adjustment and here I am. Why sulk?'

Sarah was speechless. It was like trying to argue with a maze that kept on increasing in complexity, losing her at every turn. 'Here I am', he said with such staggering self-assurance, as if she could not fail to be grateful to win such a prize.

'After all, you fought back like an Amazon warrior,' Alex told her thickly, his dark head lowering inch by inch. 'You ignored me, you ignored it all and the more you ignored what I was doing, the more I seethed . . . I discovered that the one thing I cannot stand is to be ignored.'

She didn't know what he was talking about. He appeared to be suggesting that her avoidance of him had been part of some sly, manipulative female plot to attract him and his unquenchable ego took to that idea like a duck to water. On the brink of acidly disabusing him of that notion, her parted lips met on a shocking collision course with his.

Alex groaned against her mouth and possessed it again with renewed vigour and a force of hunger that ran a scorching blaze of heat right down to her toes and back up again. She fought the effect, concentrating her mind on the picture of herself pregnant and miserable while Alex strayed to be chased, flattered and encouraged by other women.

Tearing her swollen lips from his single-minded onslaught, she gasped, 'I don't want to get pregnant.'

'No chance,' Alex muttered in thickened agreement.
'Not for at least a year. It might curb *this*...'

He teased her mouth with his tongue, mimicking a far
more intimate penetration, and she quivered, every limb
boneless, every nerve-ending begging for more, and,
feeling that, she wanted to scream. If she had had the
capability to lie there like a waxen dummy, unresponsive
to his seduction, Alex would have left her alone. And
she wanted Alex to leave her alone, didn't she...?

One hand was in his silky hair, the other curved round
his warm shoulder, rejoicing in the silky smoothness of
his skin...and she didn't know how either had got there.
Her body appeared to be totally detached from her brain.
It had broken out all on its own. And she *wanted* to
touch him, she realised in dizzy shock, wanted so badly
to be in his arms that the thought of not being there, of
actually tearing herself free, physically hurt.

Rolling over, Alex shed the remainder of his clothing
in a couple of fluid movements. Dark golden eyes drew
her. 'Come here,' he urged softly and opened his arms.

The shock of even that brief separation had chilled
her. She shifted across the bed so fast, she made it in
record time.

Alex tugged her down on top of him and curved two
lean hands to her cheekbones. 'At last,' he breathed, as
conscious of that tiny instant of surrender as she was.
'Don't ever deny me again.'

She felt his power over her and her mind recoiled from
that reality. It was just sex and if she really wanted to
fight it she could—of course she could, a voice inside
her head protested. But she trembled in his grasp, sen-
tenced to stillness by the charismatic lure of his magnetic
gaze. He held her there by sheer force of superior will.

'Ever,' he repeated persistently.

Utter surrender, that was what he demanded. She knew it, she hated it and yet she still did not fight him.

'And you'll find out just how generous a lover I can be,' Alex completed.

Her brain had turned to mush. A long-fingered hand was skating down her arching throat into the valley between her breasts. His thumb rubbed against a painfully taut nipple and she gasped, quivered, closed her eyes tightly against the intrusion of his. He pulled her up over him and suddenly curved his mouth to that betraying peak, the silk providing a quite inadequate barrier.

Sarah moaned in a crazy mixture of shame and excitement. Impatient hands trailed down the straps, baring her breasts. She tensing, and her eyes flew open. He engulfed a thrusting pink bud with the heat of his mouth and she cried out, lashed and tormented by sensation, the image of his dark head against her breasts forever imprinted inside her head.

Alex spread her flat and she was breathing as though she had run a mile in a minute, boneless as a rag doll. He touched her, shaped her, caressed her and moved down her quivering length with his tormenting mouth and the kind of erotic expertise she was defenceless against.

He ran the tip of his tongue across her stomach and her thighs parted involuntarily, an ache that was sudden agony stirring and making her clutch at his hair with near frantic fingers. He knew where she ached and she stiffened in sudden shock as he touched her but, before she could obey an instinctive impulse to jerk away, his hands curved over her thighs, imprisoning her.

'No... not *that*...' she gasped.

But he didn't pay any attention to that stifled plea, and a moment later she was lost, possessed by a desire so all-encompassing, she couldn't even vocalise through it. The impossibly intimate explorations Alex was subjecting her to reduced her to a quivering, whimpering state of mindlessness quite unequalled in her slender experience.

Pleasure and the pursuit of it engulfed her in the screaming demands of her own body. She moaned, she jerked, she burned, the victim of a consuming hunger that made her nails scrape down the sheet beneath her and every part of her blaze with unbearable heat. And just when she was on the torturous edge of the fulfilment she craved Alex moved over her and drove into the honeyed welcome he had prepared for himself. Instantaneously she was thrown into a climax that threw her shivering body into spasm after spasm of hot, drugging, glorious pleasure.

Alex was watching her when she surfaced again to the world she had left behind. Dazedly, her lashes fluttered on the brilliance of his smile. He thrust into her again, slowly, purposefully, and she shut her eyes, shattered to feel the electrifying excitement awakening afresh. He made love as if there were no tomorrow and she was overwhelmed because she never ever wanted tomorrow to come. The pleasure went on and on and on and the second time she hit the same heights of fulfilment it was even better...

Sarah surfaced in the tumbled bed, wondered what day it was, where she was, who she was... Five hours in bed with Alex had made her more than a little uncertain. She had a vague memory of him dressing before she fell asleep. Dressing in haste but not so fast that he hadn't had time to survey with satisfaction the plundered, witless female still lying in his bed.

Sarah cringed. Alex had strolled out of his bedroom, positively re-energised by the completeness of her surrender. And she had smiled dizzily back at him with what lingering energy remained to her, possessed of an utterly appalling belief that Alex was so incredibly wonderful that she was blessed above all other living women.

Passion killed her intelligence. In bed, she didn't think with Alex, she merely functioned like some sort of passion toy, programmed solely to give and receive pleasure. And she didn't think she could blame her response on a teenage experience of rejection any more. It wasn't that simple. She was falling in love with Alex, falling like a brick from the top of a high building, her feelings rushing faster and faster as she headed for sure and certain devastation when she hit the ground.

Now she knew why it hurt when Alex accused her of being a liar. Now she knew why she hadn't had the strength to fight Alex off. On a deep atavistic level she wanted Alex any way she could get him. When or how could it have happened? How could she possibly have started falling in love with a male like Alex? He was the very antithesis of what she admired in the male sex.

But fantastic in bed, her wanton *alter ego* piped up smugly, and her skin burned with embarrassment because she had to live with this new side to her character, this sexually attuned side which took over when Alex touched her. Sudden hope blossomed inside her. Maybe it wasn't love; maybe it was just a physical infatuation. What did she know about love? Nothing. A severe crush at sixteen and then an emotional desert ever since. It wasn't love, she told herself staunchly, it was just hormones erupting like a volcano, having been suppressed too long.

She crawled out of bed, aching in every joint. He was oversexed. He treated her like a bimbo. He'd married her with gritted teeth and then informed her that she would make the perfect mistress... yuck! Every move she made was misinterpreted by his rampaging ego! He made Neanderthal man look like the very pinnacle of male mental development. Alex was so basic, he ought to be extinct.

But he wanted her...oh, yes, Alex wanted her...for the moment—for probably about as long as it took for him to register the fact that she was no longer a challenge. If she clung, her novelty value would shrivel up and die. Being married to Alex, she decided, was more like having an affair.

She was emerging from the nursery when Claudine and Alex's butler, Henri with the expressionless face, appeared.

'A special delivery, *madame*.' Henri extended a package to her, unusually breathless, as if he had hurried instead of strolled at his usual stately pace.

'For me?' Frowning in surprise, Sarah tore off the fancy gold paper and found a jewel case. She flipped open the lid, her eyes widening as she read the message on the card, penned in Alex's almost indecipherable scrawl. 'For the most erotic and exciting five hours of my life... I can be romantic too. Alex.'

Beneath the card was a breathtaking diamond necklace on a velvet bed. Her eyes smarted and burned. 'I can be romantic too'... Like hell he could be, she thought bitterly, painfully. What was so romantic about being rewarded for giving him a good time in bed? Neanderthal man had bombed out at supersonic speed. He hadn't a clue how to be romantic because he had never been forced to stir himself into making that amount of effort.

Conscious of politely straining heads and still hovering company, she dug the card into her pocket and extended the box for appraisal.

'Oooh!' Claudine gasped ecstatically.

'*Magnifique*,' Henri breathed, impressed to death.

'Want to try it on?' Sarah offered Claudine carelessly.

'*Non, madame*,' Claudine said in shock. 'But allow me to assist you...'

A minute later Sarah had the diamonds round her throat, for the sake of appearances. She was duly admired and then mercifully freed from her audience. She hung over Nicky's cot. 'He's not only unromantic, he's insensitive. It's as if he's paying me...you know?' A sob caught in her working throat. 'It should have been flowers or just a note or a fluffy toy or something.'

She had only just finished eradicating the streaks of mascara half an hour later when she was interrupted by Henri. A visitor. A Madame du Pré.

The woman who advanced towards her across the depth of the *salon* quite took Sarah's breath away. Very tall and slender, her smooth black hair caught back ballerina-style in a snood, her clothing just screaming designer style, she was not only beautiful, she was enviably elegant. A grave smile curved her perfect bone-structure as she extended a slim white hand. 'I am Elise. I hope I may call you Sarah.'

'Elise,' Sarah gulped. 'Please sit down.'

'I can see you are not feeling quite up to dealing with a visitor,' Elise assured her sympathetically. 'I am very sorry to intrude at such a time.'

'I had lunch ages ago,' Sarah murmured, wondering why she wasn't supposed to be up to coping with her first, indeed her one and only visitor.

Elise uttered a rueful laugh. 'I think we both know that I was not referring to the hour of the day.' Gracefully she sank down into an armchair. 'I have known Alex for so many years that I count myself a close friend of the family. If it were not for that fact, I would not have dreamt of coming here to offer you my assistance.'

Sarah settled down rather jerkily opposite, unnerved by the perfection of the woman Alex had planned to marry, her concentration lapsing. 'Sorry...your assistance?' she queried uncertainly.

'I would hate you to consider this visit of mine an intrusion.'

'Of course not. You are very welcome,' she assured the older woman manfully.

'Thank you,' Elise conceded graciously in turn and then sighed. 'If only we could have met in less fraught circumstances. Forgive me if I am blunt but I am well aware of the treatment Alex has been subjecting you to... You must be feeling so alone, so isolated, so humiliated...'

Sarah stared at her. 'Must I be?'

'Sarah...' Elise chided softly. 'When all of Paris is agog to read the latest outrageous exploit in the gossip columns, there is no need for you to feel that you have to save face with *me*. I am here truly in a spirit of friendship and concern. The newspapers are behaving atrociously, but then Alex has courted publicity with such brazen disregard for the honour of the family name, what can one expect?'

Sarah hadn't a clue what Elise was talking about. Newspapers. It dawned on her that she hadn't set eyes on a single newspaper since the morning after the wedding. Since she only read newspapers occasionally, preferring the television news or a good book, she hadn't until now missed that astonishing absence of the printed daily word. Alex courting publicity... latest outrageous exploit? Her imagination went into overdrive. She struggled to conceal her ignorance from Elise.

'Yes, what can one expect?' Sarah said with studied casualness.

'Discretion,' Elise murmured in a suitable undertone. 'And to offer you my advice may seem encroaching...'

'No, I'd be very grateful for your advice,' Sarah assured her shakily.

'Tell Alex that you will not stand for such behaviour. He may not have chosen to publicise his sudden marriage but naturally society is aware that he is a newly married man. For him to flaunt a variety of different women night after night in the most public of places is naturally conducive to the kind of media furore one can only deplore,' Elise completed with a shake of her beautiful head.

'Different women...night after night...media furore.' The key phrases lit up in illuminated brilliance inside Sarah's whirling head. And she knew then that if spontaneous combustion existed Elise would have burned alive in front of her. Kill the messenger, she thought hysterically. The enemy had come to crow.

'I am astonished that Alex should sink to such a level.'

'I'm not,' Sarah admitted through compressed lips, a shudder running through her.

Elise surveyed her with apparently troubled dark eyes. 'I am prepared to speak to Alex on your behalf and reason with him.'

'That's very kind of you but I don't require that type of assistance.' Sarah stood up, smiling so widely, her jaw ached. 'I am so very pleased to have met you, Elise. Vivien told me how deeply impressed I would be and I am.'

Faint colour mottled the perfect complexion. Elise got up. 'But I——'

'Henri!' Sarah bawled, certain he was lurking not too far away.

'I am afraid I have offended you,' Elise said, looking impressively dismayed by the concept.

'There you are, Henri!' Sarah hailed the butler with relief. 'Please show Madam du Pré out.'

'Alex will be furious when he hears of this——'

'I don't think so.'

Trembling violently, Sarah watched Elise stalk out, the picture of wounded dignity. She listened to Henri's steps returning across the vast hall, walked to the door of the *salon* and lifted her head high. 'I want to see the last two weeks' newspapers.'

Henri perceptibly paled. 'All of them, *madame*?'

'I think you know the relevant ones, Henri,' she conceded tightly and then turned away.

Everybody knew ... everybody had known but her.
That was what Vivien had been shouting at Alex about!
And Alex had actually believed she knew as well. 'The
more you ignored what I was doing, the more I seethed,'
he had said. Claudine brought the newspapers in a fat,
well-thumbed bunch. The entire staff had been poring
over them and feeling so incredibly sorry for the new
bride, linked in misery to a groom behaving like a rutting
stag within twenty-four hours of the wedding.

Nothing could have prepared Sarah for the agony of
seeing the first photo. It dug cruel fingers into her heart.
Alex, dining with a blonde; the next one was of Alex
dancing with a brunette. She stopped there, looked no
further. She was choked with outrage, savaged by pain.
Alex had forced her to share his bed on their wedding
night and had then gone out to make an outsize fool of
her in public. He had told her she would need buckets
of humility to stay married to him and he hadn't been
exaggerating one little bit.

In turmoil, she sat there, ripped apart by a sense of
betrayal so powerful, it blocked out all else. This was
the man she had spent five hours in bed with. She was
so shattered she couldn't even cry. 'You will lie down
for me whenever I want,' he had said. And she had.

Henri was hovering when she glanced up numbly. He
passed her the phone. It was Vivien, chattering gaily
about how lonely she was in her apartment and how
much she would love Sarah to go out to dinner with her.
'Love to,' Sarah said numbly.

An hour later, Henri appeared again. This time he
passed the phone as if it were an offensive weapon.
'Monsieur Terzakis,' he told her.

Sarah snatched at the phone like a madwoman, suddenly galvanised into life again by the power of sheer
shuddering rage and hatred.

'How do you feel?' Alex purred in a tone of deeply
intimate recollection.

'Gobsmacked!'

'I don't think I know that expression...'

'I saw my first newspaper in thirteen days this afternoon,' she said sweetly. 'And then I went on to my second old issue. Gobsmacked,' she said again in the simmering silence echoing from the other end of the line.

'You didn't...know?' Alex asked sounding astoundingly hesitant.

'And I was the only person who didn't, wasn't I?' she said fiercely, tears suddenly springing to her eyes.

'I can explain——'

Sarah wasn't listening. 'What Vivien may have done to your father is *nothing* to what I am capable of.'

'I'm coming home——'

'I won't be here...I'm going out on the town tonight!' Sarah blazed down the receiver, her fingers crushing it. 'You want war, you got it. If you can dance till dawn, so can I! If you can sleep around, so can I! In fact there is nothing you can do to me, you sneaky, hateful toad, that I can't do back more nastily, more publicly and more painfully! The name of Terzakis will be a byword for scarlet woman! You'll be down on your knees for a divorce by the time I'm finished with you!'

'If you go out tonight...if you *dare*,' Alex was growling incredulously.

Sarah cut the connection. Dinner with his stepmother—whoopee, wouldn't that make him sweat when he found out? And then she astounded herself by bursting into floods of tears, the false edge of anger suddenly swamped by the most suffocating misery she had ever experienced. Dear God, why had she said all those utterly stupid, childish things? Why had she stooped to his level? Because she had wanted to hurt back...because she loved the swine. And how could she *love* someone like that? How could any sane woman love a monster?

CHAPTER NINE

'You had the rat for twenty years...how come you didn't poison him?' Sarah muttered feverishly, downing another mansized slug of pink champagne. 'How come you didn't instil some basic moral principles with the aid of a whip and a chair?'

Vivien looked eaten by guilt. 'I never thought Alex would behave like this,' she said for the twentieth time. 'He's gone off the rails. Damon was always the one with the roving eye.'

'Alex sought safety in numbers...and Olive Oil.' Sarah referred to Elise with venom.

Vivien chuckled. 'Imagine you having the nerve to throw her out!'

'She had her five minutes of fame first and boy, did she enjoy it,' Sarah recalled, reaching for her glass again, ignoring the food untouched on her plate. She wondered how much champagne it would take to wipe out the horrible images inside her head. Teetotal all her life, driven to drink by Alex.

'Nicky isn't your child,' the little blonde woman said abruptly. 'He isn't Alex's either, is he?'

Sarah stared across the table in a state of frozen animation.

'Andy gave it away—didn't even know she'd done it,' Vivien sighed. 'He's Damon's little accident...am I right?'

'I just can't talk about this to you, Vivien,' Sarah whispered in horror.

'Look, I know,' Vivien stressed. 'I wanted so badly to believe that my suspicions were wrong, but Alex...'

It just didn't make sense. But if you aren't that baby's mother, who is?'

'My sister. She's dead.' And Sarah couldn't stop it— the whole story just came tumbling out, short, unsweet, shorn of all but the most basic details.

'Their marriage was in deep trouble last year,' Vivien told her, and reached for her hand to squeeze it gratefully. 'Thank you for not treating me like an idiot. Sooner or later Andy will tell me and I'll be prepared. I won't badmouth Damon and put my feet in it and I won't tell anyone that I already knew. Now, let's talk about something else.'

'How do I go about getting a divorce and keeping Nicky?' Sarah enquired, happy to oblige.

Vivien's eyebrows almost vanished below her feathery fringe. 'You're not thinking of *divorce*, are you?' she exclaimed in consternation.

'What else would I think about?' Sarah's voice slurred slightly.

'Strategy,' her mother-in-law supplied with enthusiasm.

'I have no desire to fight for Alex,' Sarah responded as gently as she could. 'This is a marriage of convenience that went badly wrong from the word go, not a romance that went tragically off course.'

'Let's go on to a nightclub, relax,' Vivien suggested rather abruptly, having glanced at her watch.

'Dance till dawn, stay out all night,' Sarah added facetiously.

'If you like,' Vivien beamed, encouraged by such remarks.

Sarah followed her into the chauffeur-driven limousine awaiting them outside. She leaned back, smiling fixedly, while Vivien rabbited on about how to hold on to her marriage. What marriage? she almost said before she learnt to block her ears and switch off. In the grip of grief and bitterness, she had demanded that Alex marry her. She had been blind to the threat that Alex might have a hidden agenda. In retrospect that seemed incredibly dim of her, nor was it at all surprising that disaster had resulted. Now it was time to stop drifting with the tide, pick herself up out of the debris and sort her life out. But what about Nicky? a little voice screamed, throwing her back into chaos.

Her jangling emotions felt savaged. And she blamed herself entirely for her state of maudlin misery. She had fallen in love with Alex. In one blow, she had deprived herself of the ability to fight back. Love had addled her wits, decimated her pride and torn her in two. If she hadn't loved Alex, if she hadn't succumbed to the lure of all that dark Greek machismo, she would have been untouchable.

'Freshen up your lipstick, look bright and happy,' Vivien instructed chirpily.

The nightclub was noisy, full of a crush of people and heaving bodies on the dance-floor. As she slid behind a table, she noticed a little man staring at her over the back of his seat. As fast as she noticed his interest, he hurriedly turned away again.

'Have another drink!' Vivien told her loudly.

Another bucket of pink champagne had magically appeared. Vivien stuffed a roll of notes into the waiter's hand, pressed the glass across to Sarah helpfully. Sarah obliged out of politeness and surveyed her surroundings, admitting that she was on the way to getting very drunk while knowing that a lady did not do that— ever.

'Sarah!' Vivien exclaimed, clutching her arm. 'This is Stefan.'

'Ste—what?' Sarah noticed the lights from the floor had been blocked by a very large presence. Wide-eyed, she took in the enormous young man smiling widely at her from the other side of the table. He looked like a

Chippendale, all blonde hair and muscles and white teeth.

'He's an escort . . . I've hired him for the night.'

Sarah giggled. She just couldn't help it. Stefan settled into the place Vivien had vacated.

'V-Vivien?' Sarah gasped.

Vivien disappeared at supersonic speed into the crush.

Stefan smiled pleasantly. Sarah felt it was only fair to smile back before she told him that there had been a misunderstanding and that it really wasn't his fault that her mother-in-law was a maniac. Then it happened. An alarming flash of light blinded her. The photographer lowered his camera. The little man with the weasel face she had seen earlier retreated fast.

'You like to dance?' Stefan asked in a guttural mid-European accent.

Her legs wouldn't hold her up. Vivien swam back to their table, brimming with triumph. 'Where would you like to go next?'

Sarah stood up. 'Home . . . alone.'

'Sarah! If you go home early that will give the game away.'

Sarah had meant home as in London. 'Vivien, you shouldn't have done this.'

'I had to do something!' Vivien told her vehemently.

'I need some fresh air. Goodnight,' she told Stefan.

'Didn't you like him?' Vivien whispered fiercely as Sarah forced her passage through the crowds.

'Did you set up the photo session?' Sarah asked once they were out on the pavement, reeling slightly as the air hit her.

'Of course. If nobody knows what Alex's wife looks like, how can they catch her *in flagrante delicto*?'

Oh, dear God . . . Overpowered, Sarah sank back into the limousine.

'I seem to have upset you. I was only trying to help,' Vivien persisted in a pained tone.

Sarah just groaned out loud. She dropped the other woman off at her apartment and then settled back again, acknowledging that she was not feeling up to facing Alex just yet, assuming he had come home as he had said he would... and she was so darned sleepy.

'Could we drive around for a while?' she asked the chauffeur.

She fell asleep, slowly sinking down along the back seat into a supine position.

Cold air woke her up from a semi-stupor. With immense effort, she dug her elbows back and slightly lifted her swimming head to squint at the male looming over her.

'Why the hell didn't you phone me?' Alex blazed at the chauffeur.

'Not his fault,' Sarah slurred, struggling without much success to sit.

'Where have you been?' Alex bit out, every word aimed like a bullet. 'It's three in the morning, almost dawn! You have been absent for eight hours.'

'AWOL,' Sarah giggled helplessly and slithered slowly out of the car, feet first.

'And you are paralytically drunk,' Alex seethed with naked incredulity.

Surprisingly he caught her before she fell. 'I can walk,' she said.

He was dishevelled, his hair tousled, his jawline stubbled. And he was mad. He was so mad, he could hardly articulate. Detached from him by this wonderful wall of cotton wool, she felt no pain. The rat, the treacherous, double-dealing, hypocritical swine that he was...

She made it up the steps all on her own, and headed doggedly for the stairs. She kicked off her shoes, lifted the hem of her long dress, searched for something to hold on to and a second later was swept up into Alex's arms. 'You're hurting!' she moaned because he was crushing the air from her lungs.

'If you ever do this again,' Alex swore, little tremors interfering with the normally steady tenor of his deep, dark drawl, 'I will take measures to restrain you.'

'It's the attic for me!' Sarah sang off-key.

'Where were you? Who were you with?' Alex demanded, dropping her down on to a wonderfully comfortable bed.

'Are you being *possessive*, Alex?'

'If you've been anywhere near another man, I'll kill you,' he intoned, staring down at her with paint-stripping intensity. 'You're my wife.'

'Yuck,' Sarah responded sleepily, her heavy eyelids dipping as though weights were attached to them.

When she awakened, she was alone and little men were morris-dancing inside her thumping head. My first hangover, she registered miserably, sliding out of bed and weaving a far from straight passage to the bathroom. A shower would make her feel better. She was emerging from the cubicle, swathed in a towel, white as a ghost and suffering from a raging thirst, when she noticed Alex.

'Oh, no,' she mumbled. 'Not now.'

Alex filled the doorway. She refused to look at him, concentrated on his feet.

'Shouldn't you be at the office or something?' she whispered.

'It's Saturday.'

'I thought you went every day.' He certainly hadn't spent any days at home. Her clouded gaze worked up his legs. He was wearing black jeans that hugged his long, lean thighs and narrow hips, and an Aran sweater which accentuated his dark golden skin tone and black hair. Gorgeous, so gorgeous, her knees turned weak. Accidently she clashed with hooded dark eyes and her

stomach dipped violently. The pain came back in a de-
bilitating surge.

'Who is he?' Alex displayed a newspaper, item one in
the prosecution case.

Sarah peered at the photo. Stefan and herself, caught
smiling and looking surprisingly intimate. What a joke,
she thought bitterly, and edged fluidly past Alex's incredible stillness. He could have doubled for Gina's
Greek statue, poised there with an inscrutably impassive
face and an air of earthquake-proof self-command.

'Sarah?'

She sank down on the edge of the bed. She wasn't
Vivien and she was still angry that the other woman had
placed her in so invidious a position. She ran a hand
through her tumbling hair, knowing she looked like death
warmed up. It didn't help.

'He's an escort Vivien hired and sprang on me,' she
murmured wearily. 'She also tipped off the photographer.'

'Vivien?' Alex breathed incredulously.

'Look, I really don't care whether you believe me or
not.' Sarah told him briefly what had happened, talking
to his feet throughout. Direct visual contact *hurt*.

'You didn't have to tell me that he was an escort. You
could have lied,' Alex drawled flatly after a very long
silence.

'Why?' Sarah glanced up, her emerald eyes pained,
her soft mouth tight. 'I don't play those sort of games.
What would be the point?'

He studied her, disturbingly tense, his eyes dark
glimmers of light beneath black lashes. 'Sometimes those
sort of games work on men like me.'

'That's not my style,' she admitted, dry-mouthed.

'It was Vivien's. Why did you tell me the truth?' he
demanded abruptly again.

How many lies and deceptions had Vivien practised
on his father? How many had Alex witnessed? Vivien

was fundamentally kind and caring and Alex was clearly fond of her, but it was equally clear that about the last thing Alex appeared to expect from a woman was the whole truth and nothing but the truth. He expected manipulation and manoeuvres, point-scoring and pretences, not honesty. He could not understand why Sarah should without pressure openly admit that Stefan had been an escort and the photo a rigged-up piece of farce.

'Why?' he repeated again. 'When I phoned yesterday, you said——'

She flushed. 'I talked a lot of tosh, the way you do when you're angry.'

'You put me through hell last night,' Alex muttered half under his breath, the admission dragged from him. 'I really thought you might——'

'Go and make an idiot of myself to annoy you?' Sarah sighed. 'No. I'm too staid for that.'

'You didn't look staid on the back seat of the limo,' Alex commented flatly.

'I've never got drunk before. I don't think I ever will again,' she conceded, studying the exquisite Aubusson rug beneath her feet.

Alex expelled his breath and swung away from her. She lifted her head, noted the raw tension in the set of his wide shoulders.

'I owe you an explanation for my behaviour,' he intoned harshly.

No apology, just an explanation. Well what had she expected?

'When I agreed to marry you, I did not intend to remain married for very long. That was...' he hesitated '...dishonest of me. But I was very angry at being forced to marry you in return for sharing custody of Nicky. I was also very bitter. Please understand that I have grown to love him.'

'Yes.' She was too engulfed by guilt to say anything more.

Alex swung back to her, his darkly attractive features strikingly serious. 'But he came into this world in circumstances which I personally would never have been guilty of allowing. Yet it was I who was called to pay for the offence.'

'I'm sorry.' Her eyes smarted painfully.

'But what alternative was there? Your motives may not have been entirely pure but you had more awareness of Nicky's needs than I had. I could not have brought him up on my own, and Elise,' he delivered with a wry twist of his mouth, 'would never have accepted him. I am very fond of children but I have to confess to not having had very much to do with the breed. What I am trying to say to you is that that child needs both of us and I accept that now. However, if the two of us had had access to slightly cooler tempers in the period after your sister's death, we would not now be married...'

She knew it was the truth but it was still like a knife twisting through her heart.

'But I was not prepared to leave you in charge of Nicky, thinking of you as I did then. We were so busy striking sparks off each other, neither one of us showed our true character,' Alex spelt out. 'I was determined that you would gain nothing from the marriage. I knew you were proud. I swore to break that pride.'

The colour drained from her fragile face. 'Yes.'

He vented a soft imprecation, noting her pallor. 'Hence my behaviour after the ceremony. I did not feel like a married man. I did not want to be a married man,' he confessed with grim emphasis. 'I saw marriage as something still quite far in the future, to be embraced at a time of my choosing. So I decided to marry you and get rid of you again by whatever means were within my power.'

Sarah bowed her head, her throat thickening. She had blown Alex's no doubt smoothly organised existence apart. What right did she have to resent the backlash?

Hadn't she brought it on herself? How could she demand fidelity from a man who had never wanted to marry her in the first place?

'You're so quiet.'

It was easier to shout and scream in temper, tougher to verbalise really painful emotions which Alex could only be embarrassed by. His candour was slaughtering her, she acknowledged. She had managed by extraordinary means to fall in love with a man primed from the outset to humiliate and hurt her. What was worst of all was not being able to resent that reality.

'Maybe I'm a little stunned that you're talking to me like this.' She strove for a fair approximation of an appreciative smile. It was a lost cause.

'Maybe I would like to be stunned back,' Alex murmured tautly.

He *would* be stunned if she told him how she really felt about him. Inside herself, she was dying. It was slowly sinking in on her that all that he had said about finding her sexually attractive must have been lies too! Dear God, he had run rings round her! Idiot, fool, sucker, she castigated herself fiercely. Her lack of sexual experience had been so pitifully obvious to Alex, he had made that his first target.

'Sarah...I am attempting to clear the air.' He crouched down on a level with her and reached for her tightly clenched hands. Tears were slowly trickling down her cheeks and she was in anguish that he should see them, hadn't even realised the tears were there until she felt them overflow. 'If I've hurt you, I'm sorry, but I will make it up to you.'

His hands engulfed hers with warmth. He looked really concerned. She had never dreamt that those dark golden eyes could soften to such a degree. But that her weakness should provoke his pity tormented her.

'I can,' Alex swore vehemently. 'I can make this marriage work.'

Vehemently she shook her head, arching her slender throat, willing the tears back. 'It just can't work, Alex——'

'But it has to for Nicky.'

'I love Nicky very much...but I don't w-want to stay married to you,' she said. 'This situation is unbearable for both of us. We have nothing in common.'

His lean hands had tightened as she spoke, crushing the blood supply from her fingers. 'Nicky,' he reminded her. 'And there are many facets of your character which I admire.'

What remained of her pride trickled down through a mental grating, gone forever. Her damp lashes concealed the agony in her eyes. Character traits he could admire...was that the best he could come up with? This utterly gorgeous man whom she loved, who did not love her, who wanted to stay married to her for her maternal instincts. She withdrew her hands from his, despising herself for the craving to maintain even that slight contact.

'Alex...I got us into this. Yesterday I was furious with you,' she admitted with difficulty and some under-statement. 'But I shouldn't have been and I see that now. If you want to run around with a lot of women, that's your business, because we're not really married, not in the strictest sense of the word.' She paused, disturbed by the dull coins of colour rising over his taut cheek-bones. 'Neither one of us went through that ceremony meaning what we said.'

'I did not make love to any of those women,' Alex said harshly, and reached for her hands again with un-hidden anger. 'Have you ever heard of the concept of a second chance? Here I am practically on my knees begging for that chance and you sit there like a little stone Buddha being bloody forgiving but as unyielding as a brick wall!'

Shattered by the attack, Sarah watched him spring upright and stride across the room, aggression in every line of his long, lithe body. Was it true that he hadn't made love to another woman since their marriage? None of *those* women, he had said. He might not have been to Athens but he was in Paris practically every damned day! His anger had astonished her. She realised that he was deadly serious about staying married for Nicky's benefit and frustrated by her lack of response.

'I can go and get laid anywhere I want, any time!' Alex threw up two expressive hands, shooting her a look of such volatile fury that she paled. '*Dios*...my father would have killed to marry a woman like you! But if you tell me one more time that I can screw around, I'll strangle you! Do you hear me? How can I feel married if you do not set standards for me to live up to?'

So much passion, so much fire. It fascinated her, lay at the very heart of his attraction for her. Until Alex had come into her life, she had never succumbed to any excess of emotion. She had been quiet and calm and always very, very sensible. Alex had knocked her sideways and then reached inside her to inspire an unholy passion quite beyond her control.

'You told me your standards on our wedding night,' she reminded him gently.

'But you are not the woman I thought you were then. You confused me,' Alex said with natural arrogance. 'If this marriage is to have a hope of success, certain standards must naturally be observed. I know what I am talking about.'

'Really?'

Alex's sensual mouth compressed. 'My father's relationship with Vivien was a living hell for the first few years. Infidelity breeds distrust and insecurity. Even when he had abandoned his extra-marital forays, Vivien was suspicious. They loved each other very much but that bad beginning undermined their whole marriage. Because she did not trust him, she played games...'

Keeping him on his toes, Vivien had called it.

'I could kill her for bringing those games into our marriage,' Alex confessed abrasively and then, seeing Sarah's alarm, he sighed. 'She has to be told and it is my place to do it but I will try to be kind about it.'

'She knows about Nicky... about Damon and Callie,' Sarah dropped tautly, awaiting the storm.

Alex froze, frowned, then suddenly shrugged. 'What the hell? Let Andy and Damon deal with the fallout.'

Sarah was amazed by his attitude.

'Our marriage is more important and I suppose it was inevitable that Vivien would find out,' he said dismissively.

Sarah knew she was staying now, knew she had been protesting the inevitable once Alex had made it clear that he wanted her to stay. So they would make another, more meaningful attempt at being married for Nicky's sake. Could she live with that? Her world would revolve around Alex and Nicky but she would only be a tiny part of Alex's world, she reflected painfully. The wife he would make the best of, not the wife he would have chosen, not the wife that he loved.

She took a deep breath. 'I'll stay if you want me to.'

'At least until Nicky is eighteen,' Alex told her smoothly.

The qualification so casually stated turned her stomach over sickly. Careless words that bit and hurt because they underlined Alex's emotional detachment. 'I'd like to get dressed.' Standing up, she gave him a small, tight smile.

'Why don't we take Nicky out somewhere together... like a real family?' Alex suggested abruptly.

It had been a gorgeous day. He had taken them to the town of Chinon and they'd played tourist, wandering the medieval streets in the sunlight, lunching in a superb restaurant and talking as they had never talked before. It had been curiously like being on a first date, Sarah reflected sleepily in the car on the way home. Alex had been very restrained, excruciatingly polite and considerate, and Nicky had risen magnificently to the occasion of his first family outing by dutifully eating, napping and bestowing fat smiles on them both.

Sarah went to bed at ten. Alex had disappeared into the library after a phone call. She was half asleep when he slid into bed beside her. She stole a glance at him, her heart leaping wildly behind her breastbone. He reached for her simultaneously, incandescent golden eyes literally defying her to object.

She didn't want him to touch her and he knew it. Shivering, she closed her eyes, hiding her pain and disillusionment, and knew that this was the price, this was the bottom line if she wanted to hang on to him. Alex needed sex the way she needed air to breathe. Fidelity meant that he now had to satisfy those needs in the marital bed.

She was just a *body*, and if anything had been required to prove that point his silence did so. In this new brave relationship, lies were no longer permissible, so Alex was not about to tell her how ravishingly irresistible she was. She was fanciable enough to arouse him but that was the height of her pulling power and, with a male as physical as Alex, maybe it didn't even take that much ... maybe he just fantasised about somebody else. A choked sob escaped her.

He thrust her away from him with positive violence. Her eyes flew open as he threw back the sheet and sprang out of bed.

'Alex ... you misunderstood!'

He spun back, dealing her an incredulous glance.

'I was thinking about something else ... It wasn't—I mean ...' she stumbled in desperation, knowing that the whole future he had offered her was in the balance. The tip of her tongue stole out and darted along her taut lower lip. 'I want you,' she whispered finally.

Dark golden eyes held hers in the throbbing silence and then a vibrantly amused smile curved his expressive mouth. He strolled back to the bed, closed his hands over her shoulders and took her mouth with a searing hunger that sent the blood drumming through her veins. He pressed her back and came down on her in one smooth movement.

'Prove it,' he muttered thickly, settling his hips between her parted thighs, one hand summarily dealing with the tangled silk of her nightdress, wrenching it out of his path.

She trembled, learning the heat of his arousal, filled by an intense excitement she could not deny. He kissed her again then, forcefully, almost roughly, and she tangled her hands breathlessly in his hair, kissing him back with a kind of crazy desperation, gripped by an urgency that burned.

He took her in a storm of passion, wringing every last drop of response from her quivering body. No smooth seduction this time, nothing but the raw driving ferocity of male possession. Afterwards, she was shattered by the extent of her own enjoyment. The suspicion that Alex had been out of control as well had wildly excited her. She lay in a damp tangle of limbs, her arms tightly wrapped around him.

'I'm sorry.' Alex pulled away, threw himself back against the pillows and stared up at the ceiling, a dull flush of colour darkening his hard cheekbones. 'I need a shower.'

She turned over, wondering what was wrong, afraid to ask in case he told her. Ten minutes later, he left the room and she lay sleepless in the darkness. He came back to her with the taste of brandy on his lips at some timeless stage of the night and made love to her all over again, slowly, gently, and with immense restraint. She told herself that it didn't matter that he was careful not to encroach on her side of the bed afterwards. She told herself that if she couldn't have love she would settle for sex and that she wasn't going to let herself be oversensitive in her expectations. But long after Alex was safely asleep she cried for what she couldn't have.

The following days blurred one into another. The staff were very busy preparing for the big party Alex was determined to throw. When Sarah wasn't putting on a brave show for Alex's benefit, she was with Nicky, to whom she clung more than ever, taking comfort and strength from his unquestioning love and need for her. She went shopping because Alex told her to. She bought fabulous clothes without any real pleasure.

He took her out to dinner several times, but when they were photographed he froze and looked guilty as hell. She wore the diamonds he had given her and which she had never thanked him for and, when she attempted awkwardly to make good the oversight, he brushed her words away as if they embarrassed him and she fell silent. It was that night that she began to pick up on the edge of guilt that betrayed him.

'I need you,' he would admit with a flat lack of emotion that chilled her in the dark of their bed but, even though he gave her extraordinary pleasure, he still seemed to feel the urge to apologise for that same need. He never laid a finger on her otherwise. During the hours of daylight, it was as though she were ringed by a defensive force-field, but at night it was as though he couldn't keep his hands off her and all restraint vanished. He exhausted her to such a degree that she took to sleeping in late in the mornings.

The beginning of the second week he started coming home with giant bunches of flowers and then the meaningful conversations started. He behaved as though everything about her was a source of endless fascination. He wanted to know about her childhood, her parents, every lousy job she had ever had, and her tension began to build to explosive proportions because she knew he couldn't possibly be one-tenth as interested as he was trying to pretend.

'Do you really have to try so hard to live with me?' The desperate demand just flew from her lips at the end of the second week over dinner.

He tensed, his jawline squaring. 'What do you mean?'

'You don't have to try so hard to make me feel wanted,' she murmured tautly, her shadowed eyes resting on him. 'I'd rather you were just yourself.'

Brown fingers beat a silent tattoo of tension on the polished table. His magnificent bone-structure tautened, a tinge of pallor showing beneath his sun-bronzed skin. 'I can't do anything right with you, can I?' he breathed with a ragged edge to his deep voice, his accent thicker than she had ever heard it.

'It's not that.' But how could she say to him that she found the spectacle of his obvious efforts to make their marriage work increasingly humiliating. It would go too close to the bone for both of them. An enormous lump formed in her throat. She wished she had kept her mouth shut. That much effort to give her what he believed would make her happy ought not to be condemned. She bent her head, decided she was an ungrateful bitch and fought the tears threatening.

'You like flowers in the garden but not flowers I give you. You can chatter endlessly to my servants but you can hardly bear to tell me your favourite colour. The message isn't subliminal, is it? The only place I feel even marginally welcome is our bed and why is that?'

Shaken by the storm she had ignited, the roughness of his strained intonation, she stared at him, devoured by pain.

'Why?' Alex repeated fiercely.

Because I love you...

'And you're all over Nicky at every hour of the day. He coughs and you can't get there quick enough!' Alex slung from between gritted teeth. 'In spite of the fact that we have a nanny with several willing supporters, you install a baby alarm and you get out of my bed to go to him!'

Very much taken aback, Sarah surveyed him with shocked eyes. Evidently the baby alarm in their bedroom was viewed as some kind of ultimate insult. Did he think she was smothering Nicky? Was that what he was saying? That she was threatening to turn into one of those ghastly suffocating mothers one read about? She reminded herself that Alex had probably been raised more by nannies than parents and possibly he did consider the amount of time she spent with Nicky excessive.

'I'm sorry if you think I'm taking my responsibilities too seriously.'

'If you're that obsessed with babies, why should we wait until next year to extend the family?' Alex demanded with sardonic bite, his eloquent mouth twisting as he absorbed her consternation. 'Now isn't that a wonderful idea?'

'I don't think we're ready for another child,' she blustered, wondering what on earth was the matter with him.

'You're not thinking clearly, *pethi mou*.' Alex unleashed a wolfish smile on her. 'Instead of lying there in stony silence, tolerating my regrettable sexual demands, you could maybe develop a little enthusiasm, say my name, touch me, shock me to death... After all, it would be for a higher purpose!'

Sarah was chalk-pale with mortification. 'I didn't realise... that you were dissatisfied,' she practically whispered.

'How could you? You're probably too busy reciting the multiplication tables or anticipating the excitement of Nicky's next feed!'

Without a further word, Alex vacated the table, his long stride carrying him from the room within seconds. The door thudded on his exit, and Sarah's cup of coffee blurred out of focus. She looked down at his empty seat and swallowed hard. He had noticed the difference, the difference she had been too self-conscious even to admit inside her own mind. She felt different with Alex now, hadn't realised in her naïveté that he would feel it too. No longer secure in the belief that Alex found her ravishingly seductive, she was more shy, more tense, more inclined to... just let him get on with it, the admission slunk in, and she reddened miserably.

She accused him of trying too hard and he accused her of not trying at all. 'I can't do anything right with you, can I?' There had been very real pain and frustration in that statement. He believed that she was concentrating too much on Nicky, not enough on him and therefore not enough on their marriage. Was that true? It was certainly true that she had been cowardly, too busy saving face to risk her shattered pride by making any advances of her own, forcing Alex to make every move. No wonder he was fed up to the back teeth with her. She had been so afraid of him guessing that she was hopelessly in love with him, so sunk in self-pity, she had been selfish and unresponsive.

Tonight she would be different, she swore in desperation. Tonight she would forget all those silly, self-indulgent insecurities which she couldn't afford to harbour if this very shaky marriage was not to fall apart at the seams. Then where would she be? she asked herself. She loved Alex. The prospect of life without Alex filled her with horror. It was incredible how fast her priorities rearranged themselves when she was faced with that threat.

She had a couple of glasses of wine to bolster her courage. By the time she had finished perfuming and preening herself in the bathroom, she was feeling wanton, daring, and the very last thing on her mind was Nicky's next feed. She even disconnected the baby alarm. Then, slipping on the satin *peignoir* that matched her slinky nightgown, she went off to find Alex.

He was on the phone in the room he used as an office, his back to the door, and he was laughing, so he didn't hear the door opening.

'Yes, Elise. But... it would be a little awkward if you came here... Yes, I'm glad you understand the situation. The ice is very thin right now. Yes, I know it's my own fault but do you really have to keep on reminding me?' he groaned. 'No, she still hasn't mentioned it. Why not lunch tomorrow? No, not a restaurant, definitely not. We can use my apartment. No, of course it won't make her suspicious... how could it? Sarah doesn't even know I have an apartment in Paris...'

Her heart in her mouth, Sarah closed the door so quietly and so carefully that she felt as if she was moving in slow motion. She didn't remember climbing the stairs again. The unfaithful husband... the devious bastard, attacking her when all the time he had another woman in his life. Of course, but what better form of defence than attack? It was pitifully obvious to her that Alex was planning a divorce, but only when he judged the time right. In the meantime, he was sneaking around with Elise.

In an agony of pain, Sarah threw herself on the bed. Nothing had ever hurt so badly. Shock was coasting through her in waves. Why had Alex continued to sleep with her? Or was it only tonight that he had made his decision that their marriage was a hopeless charade? Vivien would have suggested strategy. The only strategy that Sarah could envisage was killing Alex on the grounds that, if she couldn't have him, Elise couldn't have him either.

Yes, Alex had been right. The ice was very thin right now, just the merest skim of frosting on emotions that were frighteningly primitive.

CHAPTER TEN

'DAMON and Androula will be coming to the party,' Alex announced, watching her intently with veiled eyes.

'Yes.' Sarah had no reaction. She was convinced that she was really dead and that he was breakfasting with a corpse. He could have told her the sky was green and the grass was pink and she would have agreed. All she could think about was Alex's lunchtime engagement, the knowledge that *her* husband was about to embark on an adulterous affair and that she was doing absolutely nothing about it.

He hadn't come to bed last night. He had slept elsewhere. At least he had that much decency, but her lower lip wobbled alarmingly. Why on earth was he still holding this party tomorrow? Why not make some excuse to cancel it? Why go to such enormous trouble and expense to launch socially a wife he had already decided to dump?

The post was delivered on a silver tray. There was a letter for Sarah with a London postmark. It was from a solicitor's firm and it related to...Callie's will. *Callie's will*? Her sister had had a will drawn up? It was news to Sarah. Why should Callie have had a will drawn up when she had no assets to leave? Sarah read on and began to pale.

Callie's bank account currently held an amount of money exceeding a quarter of a million pounds and this amount was increasing as large monthly payments were still entering the account. As her sister had left everything to her, would she please get in touch concerning her wishes?

'Something wrong?' Alex murmured.

Sarah's stomach had flipped. Numbly she slung the letter down the table at him and covered her face with unsteady hands. It had to be Damon's money and he must have been paying from the start. Damon had not left Callie to sink or swim without financial support as Sarah had believed. Once more, Alex had been proved right and Callie had been proved a liar, at least by omission.

'I would suggest the money be returned to source,' Alex breathed coldly.

Whatever reaction Sarah had expected, it had not been that. 'Source?' she queried.

'The legal proceedings by which we will become Nicky's adoptive parents have already begun. I do not require my brother to support a child whom I intend to bring up as my own,' Alex extended with flat emphasis.

'I wasn't thinking of that angle,' Sarah muttered, surprised that he hadn't picked up on the more basic point. 'You too think that that money must be Damon's but I didn't even know it existed. Callie didn't tell me and——'

'Whose idea was it not to cash the cheque I had given her?' Alex cut in.

'Mine, but——'

'Your sister had a little more financial wisdom than you, then,' Alex responded ruefully. 'She was thinking of the future. No doubt she thought you would object to her making use of the money, so she kept quiet about it.'

He was handling the evidence that his brother had done exactly what he had assumed he would have done with unexpected generosity. He wasn't crowing. Somehow that was no comfort to Sarah.

'The lies she told me...' she whispered helplessly.

Alex sighed. 'She lied because she loved you and cared about your opinion of her. But occasionally it can be a little trying to live with someone whose moral principles are set higher and more rigidly than your own...'

Sarah took that assurance very personally, relating it to their relationship rather than her dealings with her late sister. The blood drained from her cheeks. Did Alex find her hard to live with? Had Alex decided she was a narrow-minded prig, whose principles were set in unforgiving stone? Was that how Alex saw her and was that why Alex was turning back to Elise, convinced that there was no hope for their marriage?

'As unyielding as a brick wall,' he had called her. And hadn't she been behaving that way? The way she treated Alex did stem from one basic inner conviction...that if he didn't love her he shouldn't be making love to her. In a marriage currently at its last gasp, she had been maintaining unsustainable and unrealistic standards. Was it any wonder that Alex was on the brink of straying?

On the brink—that meant it wasn't too late. It wasn't too late to prove that she could be everything he could want within marriage, was it? But to prove that point would mean ditching not only her personal insecurities but also her pride. Could she do it? Could she turn herself into the sort of woman Alex would desire and need to the exclusion of all others? With only hours in which to achieve that miracle, she understood that she would be struggling to fulfil a pretty tall order and that it was going to take a pretty hefty demonstration to convince Alex that she could change...

Hooded dark eyes were studying her, a faint frown-line formed between his winged brows. He had spoken and she hadn't heard him. 'I said,' Alex drawled, and then, meeting her far-away eyes, his mouth suddenly tightened. He rose abruptly from behind the table. 'Forget what I said. I'll see you at dinner.'

Before Sarah could retrieve her wits and her tongue, Alex was gone. Suddenly galvanised into motion by panic, she pelted after him, but he wasn't on his own.

He was striding out of the door with his pilot on his
heels. Desperate as Sarah was, she could not quite bring
herself to proposition her husband sexually in front of
an audience.

And then he really was gone, the door thudding shut
on her hopes and her dreams and her marriage, she reflected melodramatically. Alex was off to put in a few
hours at the office before succumbing to Elise's wiles.
Olive Oil, she had called her! Talk about seriously
underestimating the opposition! Elise might not have
slept with Alex before he'd got married but evidently,
in her eagerness to extract him from his marriage, she
was prepared to get her hair mussed now.

Well, she wasn't the only one, Sarah decided in sudden
fury. She intended to put a spoke in Elise's wheels. She
was going to get in first. Cheeks hotly flushed, Sarah
tracked down Henri and asked him what time Alex took
lunch.

Henri blinked. 'It varies...'

'I need to know what time he's taking it today and I
want a car to Paris to get me there on time,' Sarah told
him. 'I want to surprise him.'

Henri smiled with sudden cunning. 'I'll find out,
madame.'

Sarah went upstairs into the dressing-room and began
to trawl frantically through the wardrobes for something suitable to wear, something seductive, something
that would come off again with the minimum of effort.
She couldn't afford to give Alex ten seconds to recall
the lunch date he was about to break. If Alex could use
sex as a weapon, as he had on their wedding night,
couldn't she?

She was ready to tear her hair out and scream when
she realised that the most basic weapon in any sensual
woman's wardrobe was missing from hers! Downstairs
she went again in a rush, straight into the kitchen to find
François, her chauffeur, with his feet up, reading a

newspaper. 'I have to go into Tours!' she announced breathlessly. 'Now!'

François could take a hint. They made it to Tours in record time. The lingerie shop she finally located offered up a wealth of choice. It took her only ten minutes to grab up those most essential missing items and then it was back home, at the same speed, to go racing up to the bathroom to commence her transformation.

By the time she made it back into the car for the drive to Paris, she was badly in need of a stiff drink to aid her recovery. It had taken so long to do her hair that *big* way on her own. Of course she hadn't been bothering since they married. She had just been washing and wearing it, not making any effort at all, hardly even bothering with make-up... As she counted up her sins, she grew increasingly appalled by such thoughtless inattention to the need to hold a man's interest. Alex was accustomed to such beautiful women. If she succeeded today, she would be spending every spare hour in the beauty salon, concealing nature's deficiencies. But it would be worth it, if it meant she kept Alex.

Every head turned as she crossed the foyer on the ground floor of Alex's office block. Sarah endeavoured not to appear self-conscious. After all, she had a coat on. The fact that she was not wearing anything very much at all underneath it did not show but she could *feel* that lack, *feel* her own shocking nakedness in the most extraordinary way.

Alex's secretary on the top floor was not, she was relieved to note, the kind of sex siren most likely to end up on her employer's lap in a weak moment. From the top of her greying hair to the toes of her flat, sensible shoes, she was efficiency personified. But she looked rather dismayed when Sarah announced her intention to lunch with her husband.

So Elise was pencilled into his diary, was she? Prepared for that eventuality, Sarah waved a supposed to be arrogant but actually rather desperate hand and said, 'Cancel any other arrangements Alex has made...and hold all calls. I don't want any interruptions.'

'But Mr Terzakis never has his calls held while he's still in the——'

'He will today!' Sarah interrupted in a rush and, lest any other arguments were coming, she hastened through the door being guarded.

Alex was on the phone behind his immaculately tidy desk. His dark head swivelled round. Sarah leant back against the door, striving to look exciting, sexually a tigress, but the amount of effort it took to fumble in search of the lock, work out its type and shoot it home without looking round or down rather spoilt the effect, she felt.

'Sarah?' Alex looked astonished.

'I'm here for lunch... I mean, I'm here in place of...' Stumbling in desperation, she fell silent, moving forward, thinking that if he found her sudden unannounced arrival that astonishing he was going to need resuscitation before she got much further.

Slowly he rose to his feet. 'What a charming idea,' he breathed, his dark brows drawing together as he studied her hectically flushed face and air of decided purpose. Then he stole a fleeting glance down at the narrow gold watch on his wrist. He dealt her a distinctly tense smile. 'Unfortunately, I'm afraid you've chosen——'

'I just couldn't wait until you got home,' Sarah broke in feverishly, his glance at his watch not having been lost on her and serving merely to stoke her tension to new heights.

His black lashes dipped lower over his intent, dark eyes, clear bemusement etched into his rigidity. 'Wait for what?' he asked with a dismal lack of comprehension.

Sarah abandoned the idea of a slow, seductive wriggle and pitched off her coat to grab his attention. 'I couldn't wait for you,' she said huskily, and embarked on the buttons of her black, narrowly cut coat-dress.

Alex's gaze had whipped over to the coat now lying in a heap and back to her fast. He seemed welded to the floor with shock. He certainly wasn't making this any easier for her, she thought painfully, her fingers turning clumsy on the buttons. In fact, the exact moment the penny dropped would probably live with her forever. Alex went from shocked to shattered. Sarah collided with incandescent golden eyes. Her breath rattled in her throat. If he laughed, she would fall apart like shattered glass. He couldn't take his eyes off her. She could see that he was making a very conscious effort to accept that this was really happening to him, with her in the starring role.

The dress gaped as she finally made it to the last button. Alex made it out from behind his desk but the damnable man was still staring at her, not doing anything.

'Sarah...' he murmured dazedly.

Desperate green eyes held his fiercely as she threw back her shoulders and let the dress slide down her arms, baring all. 'The door's locked and... I'm all yours...'

Alex's golden gaze did a lightning-fast appraisal over her pouting, pink-tipped breasts, the suspender belt, the smooth skin of her slender thighs above the black stocking-tops. '*Cristos...*' he groaned.

'You see... I can be the sort of wife you want me to be. You *won't need anybody else,*' she completed with unconscious stress.

'Never... not if you plan to enliven my working day like this,' Alex confessed raggedly, suddenly reaching for her, letting one unsteady hand slide up over her taut ribcage and close round one tantalising breast before hauling her full length against him, his other hand splaying over her bottom, curving her into contact with his rampant arousal. 'And, since no other woman has

ever done what you do to my libido, I should think
you've got me exclusively for the next fifty years...but...'

But? Every bone in her body tensed.

'...I have just one tiny phone call to make,' Alex
muttered half under his breath.

'*No!*' Elise could damned well be stood up, Sarah
thought furiously. Spearing one hand up into Alex's
black hair, she drew his head down to hers. 'I want
you...and I can't wait,' she swore with positive violence.

He paused for a split-second and then he succumbed,
suddenly, roughly, like a dam breaking its walls. He
grabbed her up to him with two bruising hands and took
her mouth with electrifying hunger, his tongue plunging
between her eagerly parted lips, demanding and taking
fire from her readily offered response. Burning alive,
Sarah gave up her last rational thought. Now *he* could
take over.

And take over he did with satisfying alacrity. By the
time she had sucked in much needed oxygen, she was
flat on her back on a sofa and Alex was standing over
her, ripping off his clothes with nothing like his usual
cool and finesse. Golden eyes were nailed to her with
such fierce hunger, she stretched shamelessly beneath the
heat and the vibrations he was putting out.

'I was going to apologise for what I said last night,'
Alex admitted in a rush. 'I was very rude and far too
impatient and you had every reason to be shocked by
what I said.'

'I took the hint, Alex...didn't I?' Sarah was starting
to enjoy herself.

'I'll be dropping hints all the time after this... *Cristos*,
I am still in shock,' Alex muttered, coming down on
her, shuddering with excitement as he came into contact
with her soft, welcoming female body, every inch of
which was programmed to seduce with willingness
and enthusiasm.

It was an hour before either of them spoke another word. A knock had sounded on the door once or twice but neither of them had heard it. Sarah was absolutely wiped out by the explosive passion that had erupted between them. It had scorched right out of control and now her face warmed a little as she remembered what she had done and what he had done and the shocking level of pleasure attained by those uninhibited diversions.

The experience had also been rather informative. Alex went crazy when she touched him even though there was nothing practised about her technique. Surely no man could manufacture that much responsive excitement? Surely it couldn't be the same for him with *any* other woman?

'You've always wanted me...just the way you said, haven't you?' she whispered, knowing the answer that would kill all her insecurities even before it came.

'Madly, compulsively...even more now,' Alex confessed, both arms wound possessively round her. 'Let's go home.'

'Home?'

Alex lifted his dark head and smiled down at her with rueful amusement. 'I really don't think I'd be worth very much if I stayed. I don't have any important appointments...'

The exact instant when he recalled that Elise had been left at his apartment was obvious to Sarah. He tensed, suddenly falling silent. Tactfully she removed her attention from him. She had won. She might not be about to boast about her methods but the bottom line was winning.

'We'll use the car, not the helicopter,' Alex said abruptly. 'I have a call to make on the way home.'

Generous in victory, Sarah asked no questions. Her marriage was intact. She had Alex and Alex was unlikely to have the energy even to consider straying in the future. They walked out of his office together. His secretary

looked a little embarrassed for them both. Sarah blushed
furiously. Alex couldn't stop smiling. That he was in an
extremely good mood was blatantly obvious to even the
most disinterested observer.

'We say hello to Nicky and then we go back to bed,'
Alex muttered thickly in her ear before they left the
building. 'Then we plan a honeymoon somewhere sunny
and secluded where nobody will interrupt us.'

The limo stopped in a street several blocks from the
Terzakis building. Alex alighted onto the pavement. 'I
hope I won't be too long.'

I hope so too, Sarah thought, suddenly tense. She
supposed it would have been too much to expect him
just to ring Elise. She noted that he had no doubt that
Elise would have waited for him even though he was
over an hour late.

He was ten minutes and he was smiling as he rejoined
her. It occurred to Sarah as Alex spontaneously reached
for her and demanded and took a long, deep drugging
kiss that Elise du Pré had to be an extraordinarily good
loser. Alex had evidently not been subjected to a storm
of reproach. His emotional high was unabated. He
flirted, he teased, he couldn't keep his hands off her all
the way back to the château. In fact he was a male transformed by... by happiness? Could her sexual response
possibly be that important to him? Sarah wondered
dazedly. But the more she looked at him, the more convinced she became that this was Alex as she had never
before seen him. So happy that he couldn't hide it.
Seemingly she could look forward to dropping into his
office and playing the sex bomb at least once a month.
If that was what it took, and it seemed that it was, never
let it be said that she shrank from her marital duty.

Henri tried to say something as they came into the
hall, wrapped round each other. Alex said something in
an aside, not paying any heed, and then the effort of
having not connected with Sarah for an entire two

minutes became too much and he swept her into his arms again, taking her mouth under his with a groan of earthy and unalloyed satisfaction.

Somebody cleared his throat loudly. Neither one of them heard. Somebody coughed. Sarah and Alex continued to kiss as though they had been apart for at least six months.

'Alex!'

In Sarah's arms, Alex froze. As he removed his mouth from hers, he muttered something abrasive in Greek and gritted in an undertone, 'Why *now*?'

Only when he drew back from her did Sarah see the young man and woman standing across the hall, both wearing similar expressions of disbelief.

'Alex?' The young woman moved forward with a tremulous smile. It was the woman in the photograph...Androula.

'I did ask you to go to a hotel, Damon,' Alex breathed abrasively.

Sarah looked at him in shock. He sounded incredibly rude.

'That isn't Sarah, Andy!' Damon hissed in visible embarrassment.

Damon didn't recognise her.

'Of course it's Sarah!' Alex retorted with raw impatience.

Damon frowned at Sarah, searching her designer-clad form, she suddenly realised, for some likeness to the unattractive, dowdy woman he recalled and, on top of the tension, it was quite simply too much for her sense of humour. She burst out laughing.

'She's like another woman,' Damon said weakly. 'I wouldn't have known her.'

Androula smiled with an amusement similar to Sarah's. 'I think we shouldn't have worried so much and we should have gone to the hotel. To think that Damon felt so guilty about you and Alex getting married!' She laughed with clear relief and linked her hand in her husband's saying, 'Look at them, Damon . . . they're lovers, not enemies!'

'Yes . . .' Damon still couldn't stop staring. 'She's gorgeous, Alex.'

Alex curved an arm round Sarah's waist. 'Yes,' he agreed with an obvious attempt to be more welcoming. 'I suppose you have come to talk. Well, I don't want to be insensitive but, to be brutally frank, I don't want a whole lot of stuff raked up that's going to upset my wife!'

'Alex!' Sarah gasped.

His cheekbones tautened, darkening in colour, and he looked down at her. 'I'm sorry, but their problems have haunted us long enough,' he muttered in an undertone. 'I don't want anything more coming between us.'

'Nothing's going to come between us. I promise,' she whispered back, her heart turning over at his obvious concern and anxiety for their relationship.

'Let's get it over with, then,' he sighed.

The four of them entered the *salon*. Alex closed the door. Damon sat down, Androula beside him. He cleared his throat awkwardly. He couldn't meet Sarah's eyes. Androula squeezed her husband's hand supportively. And finally Damon took a deep breath and spoke. 'I've been pretty inventive with the truth, Alex . . .'

'He has told many lies,' Androula rephrased ruefully.

Damon said something in Greek and suddenly Androula stood up. 'I think it would be better if I waited outside,' she said without resentment, and left the room.

Sarah sighed. 'I know you didn't let Callie down as badly as I believed.'

'I did,' Damon muttered. 'I told Alex she was a gold-digger and that there had been other men. Callie wasn't like that and you must hate me for it.'

She didn't hate him any more, she discovered. He was very immature for his age. The boyishness was more than skin-deep. He was weak. Callie had been by far the stronger personality, she acknowledged.

'You lied to me?' Alex raked in raw intimidation at his brother across the breadth of the room.

As Sarah saw Damon turn white and flinch, her patience with Alex cracked. 'Oh, keep quiet, Alex, and let him speak!'

'When Andy came over to Oxford with the children, our marriage was in a lot of trouble,' Damon admitted. 'I told her I wanted a divorce——'

'You did what?' Alex broke in.

'*Alex*!' Sarah reproved.

Alex, his strong, dark features a mask of anger, compressed his lips again.

'And Andy agreed,' Damon completed tightly, 'before she went back to Greece, before I got involved with Callie...' He met Sarah's gaze for the first time. 'I'd never met anyone like her before. I just fell like a ton of bricks for her. You know, I asked her to marry me and at the time I did mean it.'

'And I refused to believe you, *pethi mou*,' Alex murmured heavily.

'It doesn't matter now.' But she was very glad that Damon was finally telling the truth. Her love for her late sister demanded that truth.

'Callie promised me that there was no risk of her getting pregnant,' Damon continued tightly. 'She knew I didn't want that to happen and, when it did, I didn't know how to handle it. There was no way I could get a divorce quickly enough. Callie and I had a major argument. Then I went back home to see the children and...and I...well, I realised——'

'That you wanted to go back to your wife,' Sarah put in, taking grudging pity on him.

'Callie called me a useless wimp and I was in her eyes,' Damon mumbled, studying the carpet. 'I couldn't face it all. I just wished I could put the clock back. She wouldn't agree to a termination——'

Alex made a vehement sound of disgust, surveying his kid brother with flaming golden eyes of contempt. 'You asked her to marry you, you got cold feet and then you dumped her. An eighteen-year-old girl, who was in love with you! How the hell could you be so bloody selfish and irresponsible and then turn me loose on Sarah and her sister?'

Sarah saw Damon's shoulders quiver and knew he was fighting back tears. He covered his face with his trembling hands and just sat there, letting Alex's chilling recriminations beat down on him, and then Alex switched to Greek.

'That's enough . . . that is enough, Alex!' Sarah interrupted because she couldn't stand it any more. 'It's finished with. It's over. He's not the only man in the world to let a woman down.'

'Your sister died!' Alex shot at her furiously.

'Because she chose to become pregnant, not because Damon went back to his wife!' As she registered Alex's amazement, Sarah grimaced and shrugged. 'Damon did what he could. He sent her money. He didn't just abandon her.'

'Yes,' Damon confirmed, shooting her a painfully grateful look for her intercession on his behalf.

Alex expelled his breath in a thwarted hiss. Sarah wondered if he made a habit of reducing his kid brother to a speechless basket case on the brink of tears, and no longer marvelled at the lies Damon had told to save his own skin at Callie's expense. She herself had only one other question to ask Damon.

'Why did you offer to take Nicky and bring him up?'

Damon stiffened and the silence stretched. 'It was the only thing I could do to make up for her dying,' he finally conceded. 'And Andy agreed.'

'Did you really want him?' Sarah murmured tautly, skimming a silencing glance at Alex, who was visibly outraged at the turn of the conversation. 'I want to know, Damon. And I'd appreciate the truth. It'll never go beyond these walls.'

'No, I didn't want him,' Damon muttered. 'I'm really grateful that you and Alex have taken responsibility for him. It wouldn't have done much for my marriage...'

'He's done a hell of a lot for mine,' Alex murmured drily, his anger draining away as he regarded his younger brother's utterly defeated and cowed aspect. 'Luckily for you.'

'Well, you and Sarah seem to be getting on great,' Damon said uncomfortably.

'Like a house on fire,' Sarah told him gently, her bitterness completely laid to rest. He was a little boy who had never grown up and probably never would.

Damon stood up with speed, dashed a self-conscious hand across his damp eyes and headed for the door. 'Do you still want us to come to the party?' he asked.

'Of course,' Sarah said with determined cheer, since Alex was fuming at the speed of Damon's exit.

Androula was in the hall. She came straight across to Sarah with eyes that unflinchingly met hers. 'I went up to see Nicky. He's beautiful,' she said quietly. 'I don't mind. I really don't mind, because I have Damon back, you see. Can you understand that?'

Sarah could, and was relieved to see that Vivien's daughter was not hostile towards her. She watched them leave, Andy slipping her hand comfortingly into Damon's. Damon hadn't gone to see Nicky, had expressed no such desire, probably would be far happier to regard Nicky as her and Alex's son rather than as anything to do with him. It was the easy way out for him, Sarah registered ruefully, and Damon undoubtedly made a practice of taking the easy way out.

'So much for the fond father,' Alex derided, sharing her thought. 'I still had a great deal to say to him. Why did you interfere?'

'Because he couldn't take it and because I didn't want him to hate me forever because you humiliated him in front of me,' Sarah murmured quietly. 'He's weak, Alex, but he's not wicked and I think he's suffered enough. Callie's death must have been the most appalling shock to him.'

Alex lifted his hands and rested them on her slight shoulders. 'You're a very generous and intelligent woman,' he murmured tautly. 'And I owe you a very big apology for some of the things I've said about——'

'No apology required. Just as I believed Callie, you believed him.' Sarah reached up to plant a kiss on his startled mouth. 'Now make Henri feed us before I pass out,' she teased.

'I thought you were about to offer Nicky back to them,' Alex confided darkly, over the meal that was swiftly provided for them.

'I had to know how he really felt,' Sarah explained. 'Now I won't ever have to feel that I deprived him of his son.'

'Our son now,' Alex countered possessively. 'Andy will give Damon a son and they will both forget that he ever had another.'

Sarah smiled abstractedly. Not much more than a month ago, Alex had doused the candles on the table between them. He wasn't doing that tonight, and full marks to Henri. Henri patently didn't need Vivien around to read the writing on the wall.

'We'll go somewhere in the Caribbean,' Alex was saying.

Propping her chin on her hand, Sarah smothered an enormous yawn, quite content to listen to Alex making plans for a honeymoon in the sun. Her eyelids drooped lower and lower.

'I think it's time you went to bed.' She opened her eyes and found Alex grinning down at her.

'At this hour?'

'You're exhausted and we have a very big day tomorrow,' he reminded her, tugging her out of her seat.

'You're not planning on going out anywhere... are you?' Sarah muttered anxiously.

'Whatever gave you that idea?'

She was on the very brink of slumber when she fancied she heard the engine of the Lagonda Alex drove when he didn't want to be chauffeured about. Imagination, she scolded herself, and drifted off into a deep, dreamless sleep.

'Good morning.'

Focusing on Alex, Sarah had a what-a-wonderful-world-it-is feeling, a sensation merely increased by the flatteringly hungry kiss he extracted from her.

'Happy birthday,' Alex said softly.

'It's not my... Good lord, it *is*!' Sarah sat up in shock. 'I forgot about my birthday!'

'But I didn't.' Alex both looked and sounded exceedingly self-satisfied.

Sarah didn't even hear him. Her wide eyes were glued in astonishment to the large canvas propped up against the footboard of the bed. A portrait, an almost living likeness of Callie, her familiar features superbly captured in oils. 'But how...? I mean why...? For goodness' sake, where did you get it?' she demanded.

'I commissioned it from the photos,' Alex drawled lazily. 'I had to twist the artist's arm a little. She doesn't usually work at such short notice or at such speed, and never until now from photos. What do you think?'

'It's fantastic.' Sarah studied it, her eyes smarting with tears. That Alex had even remembered her birthday

would have been sufficient, but that he should have gone
to so much trouble to commission a portrait of her sister,
whose memory he had little cause to love...well, truthfully, it just knocked her sideways. 'It's so like her, so
real! You couldn't have given me anything more precious.
It's the most wonderful thing anybody's ever given me.
When did you commission it?'

'Just over two weeks ago——'

'Two weeks ago...you were thinking of my birthday
that far back?'

'I was pretty desperate to do anything possible to in-
gratiate myself,' Alex confided softly.

'With me?' Sarah looked at him in shock.

'I was ready to dig ditches to get myself into the sensitive, loving and romantic category,' Alex murmured,
leaning over her and stealing another kiss, just a tiny bit
more forceful than the last, making her head reel and
her bones melt.

'Were you?' she whispered. 'Why was that?'

'I love you.'

Incredulous green eyes locked into gold ones and
lingered. Sarah moistened her dry lips and simply stared.
'You can't...you don't mean it.'

Alex reached for her with determination. 'I love you
and all you could do was tell me I was trying too
hard...which I was, but tact might have persuaded you
to keep the thought to yourself,' he mocked, staring possessively down into her now rapt face. 'If you hadn't
come to my office yesterday, I would have been too proud
to tell you.'

'When did you fall in love with me?' Sarah prompted
dizzily.

'Before we got married. It definitely started *before*,'
Alex shared, hauling her the whole way into his arms,
smiling at her soft little sigh of pleasure as their bodies
collided in all the right places. 'Because on our wedding
night, after we had made love, I found myself thinking

afterwards what a wonderful wife you would be, and frankly that gave me such a shock, I bolted——'

'Not before you said several rather upsetting things.'

'I couldn't understand what was happening to me, so I stuck to my original plan and spent these incredibly boring evenings with other women, discovering that I very badly wanted to be with you...and that I didn't want to be rid of you, after all,' Alex confessed, running a questing hand up to cover one small, pouting breast, making her arch and moan. 'In fact I decided I never wanted to let you go but, unfortunately for me, I had loused up rather spectacularly by running round with the aforementioned other women. I swear I didn't touch one of them. I never stopped fantasising about you for a second.'

Sarah pressed her mouth dizzily to a smooth brown shoulder. 'I love you too,' she said with a sigh of glorious contentment.

'That dawned on me yesterday.'

'Yesterday?' she questioned.

'When you walked into my office I was literally...what was that word of yours? Gobsmacked—yes, gobsmacked was my reaction. There was no way you would have steeled yourself to that little display if you hadn't loved me,' Alex assured her with unhidden self-satisfaction. 'You're too shy.'

'Am I indeed?'

'And I was so happy, I totally forgot about Elise——'

'Elise?' Sarah tensed.

'I had arranged to meet her for lunch at my apartment. She was bringing the portrait.'

'Elise was?'

'She is the artist,' Alex drawled. 'Maybe when she comes to our party tonight you might try to review your opinion of Elise...'

'She painted the portrait?' Sarah was shaken.

'And, because you threw her out the last time she came calling, I didn't want to rock the boat by inviting her here in case you misunderstood our relationship or said something which might offend her.'

'I'm sorry,' Sarah muttered, beginning to wonder in dismay if she had seriously misjudged the other woman.

'Elise and I are good friends and the very fact that we never slept together should tell you that there was no great spark on either side,' Alex pointed out wryly. 'Vivien doesn't like her, but I hope that when you get to know her better you'll change your mind. Don't hold it against Elise that I once toyed with the idea of marrying her... She genuinely did come here because she was shocked by the way I was behaving.'

'I was really cut off and I didn't know what you'd been doing until she told me.'

'She understood, knew she had presumed too much, but she did only want to help. Last night I went over to her home to pick up the portrait.'

'Alex, I heard you on the phone to her the night before last and I thought you were setting up an assignation with her,' Sarah muttered in a small voice.

Alex burst out laughing. 'Is that why you came to my office?' he suddenly demanded in a choked voice, comprehension gleaming in his shrewd golden gaze. Then he was laughing again, so hard that he fell back against the pillows.

Hot-cheeked, Sarah gazed down at him. 'It wasn't funny... I was very upset!'

'Serves you right for eavesdropping,' Alex teased, pulling her down on top of him with hard hands. 'I'm not complaining. I wouldn't have missed that visit of yours for a million pounds!'

'Just one more thing... mistresses,' Sarah remarked frigidly.

'What mistresses? *Dios*... where do you think I would get the energy?'

'I know you have the energy, Alex.'

'Long gone...since before the wedding.' Alex dropped a kiss on her surprised mouth, a wonderfully tender kiss. 'I knew I was going to make love to you. I wouldn't go from one woman to another. And where would I ever find another woman as honest as you?'

'Just don't bother looking,' Sarah instructed.

'How do you feel about getting married again?' Alex probed.

'Again?'

'So that we could mean every word...in the strictest sense,' he drawled huskily.

Sarah sank into the growing heat of him. 'I think that sounds like heaven,' she conceded with a radiant smile that quite took his breath away.

'And since you're in such a generous mood,' Alex murmured in a velvety purr that made her skin tighten over her bones, 'once a year, as a sort of very special anniversary known only to us, would you——?'

'Yes,' she grinned.

'But I didn't make my request...'

'I know what you want. You're shameless, Alex.'

'Madly in love, hopelessly in love,' Alex groaned, stealing a kiss with every sentence. 'And once a year you can shock me——'

'*Only* once a year? Oh, I think I can do better than that, Alex...much...much better,' she whispered with teasing provocation while she drowned in his golden eyes. 'But you'll just have to wait and see...'

PRIZE SURPRISE SWEEPSTAKES!

This month's prize:

BEAUTIFUL WEDGWOOD CHINA!

This month, as a special surprise, we're giving away a bone china dinner service for eight by Wedgwood**, one of England's most prestigious manufacturers!

Think how beautiful your table will look, set with lovely Wedgwood china in the casual Countryware pattern! Each five-piece place setting includes dinner plate, salad plate, soup bowl and cup and saucer.

The facing page contains two Entry Coupons (as does every book you received this shipment). Complete and return *all* the entry coupons; **the more times you enter, the better your chances of winning!**

Then keep your fingers crossed, because you'll find out by September 15, 1995 if you're the winner!

Remember: The more times you enter, the better your chances of winning!*

*NO PURCHASE OR OBLIGATION TO CONTINUE BEING A SUBSCRIBER NECESSARY TO ENTER. SEE THE REVERSE SIDE OF ANY ENTRY COUPON FOR ALTERNATE MEANS OF ENTRY.

**THE PROPRIETORS OF THE TRADEMARK ARE NOT ASSOCIATED WITH THIS PROMOTION.

PWW KAL

PRIZE SURPRISE
SWEEPSTAKES

OFFICIAL ENTRY COUPON

This entry must be received by: AUGUST 30, 1995
This month's winner will be notified by: SEPTEMBER 15, 1995

YES, I want to win the Wedgwood china service for eight! Please enter me in the drawing and let me know if I've won!

Name_____

Address _____ Apt. _____

City   State/Prov.   Zip/Postal Code

Account #_____

Return entry with invoice in reply envelope.

© 1995 HARLEQUIN ENTERPRISES LTD.   CWW KAL

PRIZE SURPRISE
SWEEPSTAKES

OFFICIAL ENTRY COUPON

This entry must be received by: AUGUST 30, 1995
This month's winner will be notified by: SEPTEMBER 15, 1995

YES, I want to win the Wedgwood china service for eight! Please enter me in the drawing and let me know if I've won!

Name_____

Address _____ Apt. _____

City   State/Prov.   Zip/Postal Code

Account #_____

Return entry with invoice in reply envelope.

© 1995 HARLEQUIN ENTERPRISES LTD.   CWW KAL

OFFICIAL RULES

PRIZE SURPRISE SWEEPSTAKES 3448

NO PURCHASE OR OBLIGATION NECESSARY

Three Harlequin Reader Service 1995 shipments will contain respectively, coupons for entry into three different prize drawings, one for a Panasonic 31" wide-screen TV, another for a 5-piece Wedgwood china service for eight and the third for a Sharp ViewCam camcorder. To enter any drawing using an Entry Coupon, simply complete and mail according to directions.

There is no obligation to continue using the Reader Service to enter and be eligible for any prize drawing. You may also enter any drawing by hand printing the words "Prize Surprise," your name and address on a 3"x5" card and the name of the prize you wish that entry to be considered for (i.e., Panasonic wide-screen TV, Wedgwood china or Sharp ViewCam). Send your 3"x5" entries via first-class mail (limit: one per envelope) to: Prize Surprise Sweepstakes 3448, c/o the prize you wish that entry to be considered for, P.O. Box 1315, Buffalo, NY 14269-1315, USA or P.O. Box 610, Fort Erie, Ontario L2A 5X3, Canada.

To be eligible for the Panasonic wide-screen TV, entries must be received by 6/30/95; for the Wedgwood china, 8/30/95; and for the Sharp ViewCam, 10/30/95.

Winners will be determined in random drawings conducted under the supervision of D.L. Blair, Inc., an independent judging organization whose decisions are final, from among all eligible entries received for that drawing. Approximate prize values are as follows: Panasonic wide-screen TV ($1,800); Wedgwood china ($840) and Sharp ViewCam ($2,000). Sweepstakes open to residents of the U.S. (except Puerto Rico) and Canada, 18 years of age or older. Employees and immediate family members of Harlequin Enterprises, Ltd., D.L. Blair, Inc., their affiliates, subsidiaries and all other agencies, entities and persons connected with the use, marketing or conduct of this sweepstakes are not eligible. Odds of winning a prize are dependent upon the number of eligible entries received for that drawing. Prize drawing and winner notification for each drawing will occur no later than 15 days after deadline for entry eligibility for that drawing. Limit: one prize to an individual, family or organization. All applicable laws and regulations apply. Sweepstakes offer void wherever prohibited by law. Any litigation within the province of Quebec respecting the conduct and awarding of the prizes in this sweepstakes must be submitted to the Regies des loteries et Courses du Quebec. In order to win a prize, residents of Canada will be required to correctly answer a time-limited arithmetical skill-testing question. Value of prizes are in U.S. currency.

Winners will be obligated to sign and return an Affidavit of Eligibility within 30 days of notification. In the event of noncompliance within this time period, prize may not be awarded. If any prize or prize notification is returned as undeliverable, that prize will not be awarded. By acceptance of a prize, winner consents to use of his/her name, photograph or other likeness for purposes of advertising, trade and promotion on behalf of Harlequin Enterprises, Ltd., without further compensation, unless prohibited by law.

For the names of prizewinners (available after 12/31/95), send a self-addressed, stamped envelope to: Prize Surprise Sweepstakes 3448 Winners, P.O. Box 4200, Blair, NE 68009.

RPZ KAL